WAR!

Sensors picked up a Klingon ship closing in fast.

Behind Kirk's group the air was collecting into dazzle. Six Klingons on their stiff metallic tabards were materializing, their weapons aimed and ready.

Their leader was the first to assume full shape. His hard, slant-eyed face distorted by fury, he reached out and swung Kirk around.

"You attacked my ship!" he shouted. "Four hundred of my crew—dead! My vessel is disabled. I claim yours! You are prisoners of the Klingon Empire for committing a wanton act of war against it!"

STAR TREK 11

James Blish

**Based on the Exciting
Television Series
Created By**

Gene Roddenberry

RLI: $\dfrac{\text{VLM 9 (VLR 7–10)}}{\text{IL 7–adult}}$

STAR TREK II
A Bantam Book / April 1975

2nd printing ...... April 1975   4th printing .. November 1975
3rd printing .... July 1975   5th printing ..... August 1977
6th printing

ISBN 0-553-11417-4

Published simultaneously in the United States and Canada

Bantam Books are published by Bantam Books, Inc. Its trade-
mark, consisting of the words "Bantam Books" and the por-
trayal of a bantam, is registered in the United States Patent
Office and in other countries. Marca Registrada. Bantam
Books, Inc., 666 Fifth Avenue, New York, New York 10019.

to MURIEL LAWRENCE
for labors in the vineyard

Contents

STAR TREK 11

Preface

One of the most frequent requests I receive in the mail is to be supplied with the address of a local or national Star Trek fan club. There are so many of these, and they multiply so rapidly, that I can't keep track of them. However, sombody can, and does: the Star Trek Welcommittee.

This describes itself as a central information center to answer fans' questions about Star Trek, and to provide new fans with complete information about Star Trek and Star Trek fandom. It is a nonprofit service organization—*not* a club to join—with 105 volunteer workers in 23 states (plus representatives in three other countries) who devote their time and efforts to answering such questions. They add:

"Few fans realize all that is really available in the world of Star Trek: over 100 clubs, about 80 fan magazines, 14 books, 5 conventions annually, and many products.* That's where STW comes in—we can give you information on all of them, plus ST technology, penpals, trivia, fans in your area, ST actors, details of the making of ST (live actor or animation), revival efforts, details of the various episodes . . . Whatever your question on Star Trek or Star Trek fandom, chances are we've got the answer— or can get it for you. Write us. Please enclose a self-addressed stamped envelope when requesting information."

* These figures are as of Sept. 26, 1973. They must be much larger now; certainly there are more books!

11

The Chairman is Helen Young, and the address is:

Star Trek Welcommittee
c/o Shirley Maiewski
481 Main St.
Hatfield, MA 01038

I know nothing more about the organization than what you see above, but you risk no more than a couple of stamps (or an international reply coupon) by directing your inquiry there. The depth of *my* ignorance of the kind of information they offer is almost bottomless; I just write the books.

Another question which has become more and more frequent is, "What are you going to do when you run out of ST scripts?" And the most usual suggested answer is that I turn to adapting the animated episodes. Thanks very much, but (as probably many of you already know) that job is now being done by another writer, from another publisher. And that's probably just as well, for I have never seen a single one of the animated episodes; they haven't turned up in England yet.

Well, what *am* I going to do? The problem is still several books in the future and the solution isn't entirely in my hands. A number of letters have asked for another ST novel, like SPOCK MUST DIE!, and I'd like to try that. It was certainly fun the first time. Also, I've another idea, which I'm keeping a secret until I'm sure both Paramount and Bantam like it. I'm sorry to be so vague, but publishing is like that; a chancy business.

Though I've said more than once that I can't answer individual letters, I still get some claiming to have read all the books and nevertheless requesting such answers. The record for sheer ingenuity thus far goes to a fan who said he realized that I couldn't reply, but I at least could show that I'd read his letter by arranging the next batch of stories in a certain order, or at least dedicating the book to him.

Well, now he knows I did read it. And in case anybody else needs to know how I work: I arrange the stories in what seems to me to be the most effective order, as part of my duty to the readers as a whole. (To take a simple example, there were several scripts in which Captain Kirk was presumed dead. It would be bad editing to include two such stories in the same book.) As for dedications—well, like almost all other authors I know, I dedicate my books only to personal freinds old and new, to people who have helped me to be better as a writer, and to others I have learned to love. I mean this as an honor, whether the dedicatees take it as one or not; for a book takes time and care and skill to write, even if it turns out to be bad, so a dedication must be a gift from the heart . . . And when I can't think of someone who might particularly like a book of mine, I don't dedicate it to anyone. I hope that's clear, for I don't know how to explain it any better. I have no more friends and loved relatives than anybody else, and don't hand out dedications at random.

I hope you won't think this ungracious of me. In the meantime, let me repeat yet again: I do read *all* your letters, I'm glad to have them, and hope you'll go right on sending them. That's why I give my address. Your welcome enthusiasm gratifies me more than I can say. But I can't answer them. I have received, quite literally, thousands of them and had I replied to them all—as I tried to do during the first year—I'd have had no time to write any more books!

Finally: I've often been asked what other books I've written besides these. I'm flattered to be asked this, but there are more than 30 others and I've lost track of some of them myself. Those that are still available in English are listed in an annual volume called *Books in Print*, which you can find easily in your local library, and your librarian will help you to run down any that sound interesting. And, of course, I hope you'll like the ones you find.

JAMES BLISH

Treetops
Woodlands Road
Harpsden (Henley)
Oxon., U. K.

What Are Little Girls Made Of?

(Robert Bloch)

That day the efficiency of the *Enterprise* bridge personnel was a real tribute to their professionalism. For a human drama was nearing its climax among them, the closer they came to the planet Exo III.

Its heroine was the Starship's chief nurse, Christine Chapel. She stood beside Kirk at his command chair, her eyes on the main viewing screen where the ice-bound planet was slowly rotating. Touched by the calm she was clearly struggling to maintain, he said, "We're now entering standard orbit, Nurse."

A flicker of her nervous anticipation passed over her face. "I know he's alive down there, Captain," she said.

Kirk said, "Five years have passed since his last message." It seemed only decent to remind this brave, loving, though perhaps vainly hoping woman of that sinister fact. But she answered him with firm certainty. "I know, sir. But Roger is a very determined man. He'd find some way to live."

Uhura spoke from her panel. "Beginning signals to surface, Captain."

"Run it through all frequencies, Lieutenant." Kirk

rose to go and check the library computer screen. Spock, concentrated on it, said, "Ship's record banks show little we don't already know. Gravity of the planet one point one of Earth, sir. Atmosphere within safety limits."

"But surface temperatures are close to a hundred degrees below zero," Kirk said.

Spock, too, was conscious of the woman who was patiently awaiting her moment of truth. He lowered his voice. "It may have been inhabited once, but the sun in this system has been steadily fading for half a million years." He hit a switch. "Now for Doctor Korby, the hero of our drama, Captain . . ."

Onto the computer screen flashed a small photograph of a distinguished-looking man in his vital mid-forties. There was a printed caption beneath it and Spock read it aloud. "Doctor Roger Korby, often called the 'Pasteur of archaeological medicine.' His translation of medical records salvaged from the Orion ruins revolutionized immunization techniques . . ."

"Those records were required reading at the Academy, Mr. Spock. I've always wanted to meet him." Kirk paused. Then, he, too, lowered his voice. "Any chance at all that he could still be alive?"

Grave-faced, Spock shook his head. He switched off the photograph; and Uhura, as though confirming his negative opinion, called, "No return signal, Captain. Not on any frequency."

"One more try, Lieutenant." Kirk returned to the waiting woman who had heard Uhura's report. She said, "His last signal told about finding underground caverns . . ."

Her implication was only too obvious. Korby had sheltered in the caverns so deeply no signal could reach him. He was safe. He *was* still alive. Kirk, remembering how it is to be tortured by a hopeless hope, said gently, "Christine, since that last signal, two expeditions have failed to find him."

Uhura, making her second report, called, "I've run all frequencies twice now, Captain. "There's no—" A blast of static crackled from all the bridge speakers. It subsided— and a male voice, strong, resonant spoke. "This is Roger

Korby," it said. "Come in, *Enterprise*. Repeating, this is Roger Korby . . ."

Christine swayed. Reaching for the support of Kirk's command chair, she whispered, "That's—his voice . . ."

It spoke again. "Do you read me, *Enterprise*? This is Doctor Roger Korby, standing by . . ."

Kirk seized his speaker. *"Enterprise* to Korby. Thank you. We have your landing coordinates pinpointed. Preparing to beam down a party." He smiled up at Christine. "It may interest you to know that we have aboard this vessel—"

Korby's voice interrupted. "I have a rather unusual request, Captain. Can you beam down alone, just yourself? We've made discoveries of such a nature that this extraordinary favor must be required of you."

Astounded, Kirk took refuge in silence. Spock joined him, torn between his respect for the great scientist and the unprecedented demand. Cocking a brow, he said, "Odd. To say the least . . ."

"The man who's asked this is Roger Korby," Kirk said.

Spock spoke to Christine. "You're quite certain you recognized the voice?"

She laughed out of her great joy. "Have you ever been engaged to be married, Mr. Spock? Yes, it's Roger."

Kirk made his decision. Hitting the speaker button, he said, "Agreed, Doctor. However, there will be *two* of us." He nodded to Christine, passing the speaker to her.

"Hello, Roger," she said.

There was a long pause. Then the unbelieving voice came. "Christine . . . ?"

"Yes, Roger. I'm up here."

"Darling, how . . . what are you . . ." The voice poured excited enthusiasm through the speaker. "Yes, by all means, ask the Captain to bring you with him! I had no idea, no hope . . . Darling, are you all right? It's almost too much to credit . . ."

"Yes, Roger," she said. "Everything's all right. Now everything is just fine."

The anxious tension on the bridge had given way to a sympathetic delight. Kirk, feeling it, too, recovered his

17

speaker. "We're on our way, Doctor. Be with you soon, both of us. Kirk out."

He made for the bridge elevator, followed by the radiant Christine.

They materialized in a rock cave. It was primitive, unfurnished. Beyond its rough entrance there stretched an unending snow-world; a world as white as death under its dark and brooding sky. Its horizon was jagged, peaked by mountains. In the half-twilight of the planet's dying sun, Kirk could see that they were shrouded in ice, cold, forbidding. It was a depressing arrival.

"He said he'd be waiting for us," Christine said.

Kirk also found the absence of welcome strange. He went forward to peer deeper into the cavern; and Christine, touching one of its walls, hastily withdrew her chilled fingers. Kirk, cupping his hands to his mouth called into the darkness, "Doctor Korby! Korby!" The rebounding echoes suggested a long extenstion of distance beyond the cavern.

He was aware of a sudden uneasiness. "I suppose it's possible," he said, "that we hit the wrong cavern entry." But the supposition didn't hold up. The beamdown coordinates had been checked with Korby in the Transporter Room. And Spock was right. Korby's request *had* been odd. He detached his communicator from his belt. "Captain to *Enterprise.*"

"Spock here, sir."

"Beam down a couple of security men," Kirk said.

"Any problems, Captain?"

"Some delay in meeting us, Mr. Spock. Probably nothing at all. Kirk out." He motioned to Christine to join him at a wall to leave the cave's center open for the beamdown. "Getting up here to us may be taking more time than the Doctor estimated," he told her. "The corridors of this place may go deeper than we know."

She said, "Thank you, Captain. I'm trying not to worry."

He felt distinct relief when crewmen Matthews and Rayburn sparkled into materialization. Spock had seen to it that they were both fully armed. "Maintain your position here in this cave, Rayburn." Turning to Matthews, he add-

18

ed, "Nurse Chapel and I are going to investigate a little further. You'll go with us."

They found the narrow passageway that led out of the cave. They found it by groping along a wall. It slanted downward. The inky blackness ahead of them endorsed what the echoes had suggested. The passageway could divide itself into many unseen and distant directions.

The light grew still dimmer. Abruptly, Kirk halted. "Stop where you are," he told the others. He stooped for a stone and flung it into what he'd sensed lay right before him—an abyss. They could hear the stone rebounding from rock walls. Then there was silence—absolute. Christine had clutched at Kirk's arm when a light beam suddenly blazed at them, blinding them in its searchlight glare. Kirk jerked his phaser out. As he shielded his eyes with his left hand, a figure stepped in front of the light, a featureless shadow.

Christine hurried forward. "Roger!"

Kirk grabbed at her. "Careful! That drop-down . . ."

The figure stepped to what must have been a light-switch panel. The glare faded to a fainter light that revealed the rather ordinary face of a middle-aged man. Christine stared at him in mixed surprise and disappointment. It wasn't Korby. Kirk adjusted his phaser setting and stepped up beside her just as recognition broke into her face.

"Why, it's Doctor Brown!" she exclaimed. "He's Roger's assistant!" Identifying the man for Kirk, she rushed toward him, crying, "Brownie, where's Roger? Why . . . ?"

She never finished her sentence. Behind them, Matthews shrieked, "Capt—! Ahhhhhhhhhhhhh : . . hhh . . ."

The scream died in the depths of the abyss. Then there was only the clatter of stones dislodged by Matthews' misstep.

Sickened, Kirk pulled himself out of his shock. He went to his knees, edging himself dangerously near to the pit's rim. Pebbles were still falling from it into the blackness below. Brown joined him. "Careful . . . please be careful," he said.

Kirk rose. "Is there any path down?"

"There's no hope, Captain. It's bottomless."

Though Doctor Brown had warned of peril from the pit, he did not mention the momentary appearance of a huge, hairless nonhuman creature on the other, shadowy side of the pit. Perhaps he didn't see it. It remained only for a second before it was gone, a monstrous shadow lost in shadows. Instead, he said sympathetically, if unhelpfully, "Your man must have slipped."

"Any chance of a projection? a ledge of some kind?"

"None, Captain. We lost a man down there, too. Listen . . ." He reached for a heavy boulder and heaved it over the pit's edge. There was the same crashing of rebound—and then the same absolute silence.

"Unfortunate," Brown said. "Terribly unfortunate. Doctor Korby was detained. I came as rapidly as I could."

"Not soon enough," Kirk said.

He looked at Brown in his worn lab clothing. One learned composure in the presence of human death, if you lived with its daily threat for five years. His voice had sounded regretful. Was he regretful? Was he composed? Or was he cold, numb to feeling? Kirk could see that the weeping Christine had also sensed a certain peculiarity in Brown's response to Matthews' death.

She wiped her eyes on her uniform sleeve. "Brownie," she said suddenly, "don't you recognize me?"

"Explain," Brown said.

"You don't recognize me" she said.

"Christine, you look well," Brown said. He turned to Kirk. "My name is Brown. I am Doctor Korby's assistant. I presume you are Captain Kirk."

Something was definitely askew. Christine had already named Brown as Korby's assistant. And the man had addressed Kirk as "Captain" several times. Why did he now have to "presume" that he was Captain Kirk? Christine's uncertainty was mounting, too. Her eyes and ears insisted that Brown was indeed her old acquaintance—but the feeling of an off-kilter element in his present personality persisted. Of course, Time and harsh experience *did* make changes in people . . .

Kirk had returned to the pit's edge. "He's dead, I assure you," Brown said. "Come. Doctor Korby will be waiting." He moved over to the searchlight panel to turn a couple of switches. Lights came on further along the corridor.

Kirk walked back to Christine. "You do know him well, don't you? This Brown is the Brown you remember, isn't he?"

She hesitated. "I—I suppose existing alone here for so long . . ."

Kirk reached for his phaser. Then he snapped open his communicator. "Captain Kirk to Rayburn."

"All quiet here, Captain. Any problems there, sir?"

"We've lost Matthews. An accident, apparently. Tell the *Enterprise* to have a full security party stand by."

"Yes, sir."

"And inform Mr. Spock that we will both report in at hourly intervals. If you and I lose contact—or if he fails to hear from either of us—the security force is to be beamed down immediately. Kirk out."

He heard the snap-off of Rayburn's communicator. He couldn't hear what followed it—Rayburn's choking gurgle as the hairless creature's great arm lunged from the darkness to encircle his throat.

"This way, please," Brown was saying. "The illumination is automatic from here on."

It was a long walk. Brown appeared to feel a need to install himself as the interpreter of Korby's work. He dissertated. "The doctor has discovered that this planet's original inhabitants were forced to move underground as the warmth of their sun waned. When you were his student, Christine, you often heard him say that freedom of choice produced the human spirit. The culture of Exo III proved his theory. When its people were compelled to move from light to darkness, their culture also became choiceless, mechanistic. The doctor has found elements in it that will revolutionize the universe when removed from this cavernous environment."

The prediction struck Kirk as slightly grandiose. Polite Christine said, "That's fascinating."

"I thought you'd be interested," Brown said. "We have arrived, Captain."

The place of their arrival was a large and luxurious study. Though its walls were of rock, they were so finely polished they conveyed an impression of massive grandeur. Modern taste had been sensitively superimposed on the foundations constructed by the ancient race. In their five years of underground life, Korby and his staff had clearly undertaken to make themselves comfortable. And well supplied. There were huge cabinets of gleaming scientific instruments, archaeological tools, favorite artifacts found and cherished. Odd-looking doors led out of the room into other unseen ones. In one corner was a dining area complete with tables and chairs.

One of the doors opened. A girl came in, pale, slim, dark-haired. There was a serene innocence in her face that merited the word "lovely." Her lips moved in a smile that exposed her perfect teeth.

"I'm Andrea," she said. "You must be Christine. I've always thought it was a beautiful name."

Christine was unpleasantly startled. Youthfully innocent she might be, but the girl was nevertheless a woman. And why she was serving as hostess in Korby's personal study was a question his affianced wife was obviously asking herself.

Andrea was good as her job. She turned the lovely smile to Kirk. "And you must be Captain Kirk of the Starship *Enterprise*. I can't tell you how we appreciate your bringing Roger's fiancée to him."

Christine stiffened at the use of Korby's first name. "I don't remember Doctor Korby's mentioning an 'Andrea' as a member of his staff."

The smile didn't waver. "You are exactly as Roger described you. No wonder he's missed you so."

Such awareness of Korby's intimate emotions did nothing to alleviate Christine's growing resentment. Kirk, conscious of it, said, "Where is Doctor Korby?"

"Here, Captain." A strong-faced man, easily seen to be the man of the *Enterprise* photograph, had emerged from another door. Kirk was absurdly reminded of a theatrical buildup to the star's entrance. That Korby *was* the star, there was no mistaking. Kirk, himself accustomed to command, recognized the self-assurance in another commander. Korby, his hand extended, said, "I've been looking forward to meeting you."

Kirk had lost a crewman to a brutal death. He didn't like Brown. Nor had he lost his heart to Andrea. Ignoring the hand, he contented himself with saying, "And I to meeting you, sir."

"Roger . . ." Christine said.

"Christine . . . darling . . ."

She went to him. He bent to kiss her outstretched hands. Kirk, still wary, saw the honest joy in both their faces. It was a reunion that recovered two relationships—the intellectual bond of teacher and student, the bond of physical love between man and woman. Both loves still lived after all the years apart. So much was clear as they embraced—an embrace restrained in the others' presence but a double reunion that was real.

Christine lifted her head from his shoulder. Misty-eyed, she said, "I knew I'd find you."

He drew her back. "Forgive me, Captain. It's been a long time."

"There's no need to apologize, sir."

"The captain lost a man in the caverns, Doctor," Brown said.

There was no doubt of the horror on Korby's face. He released Christine to whirl on Brown. "What? How did it happen?"

"The pit near the outer junction. The edge must have given way."

Visibly shaken, Korby was silent. Then he spoke. "Captain, what can I say? I should have been there. I know the passages so well. I am sorry—so sorry."

"It isn't your fault, Doctor." Kirk had his communicator out. "Captain to Rayburn," he said. "Rayburn, report." As he waited for Rayburn's voice, he turned back to Korby. "I'll have to call my ship on a security confirmation. If you have any cargo requirements, any special needs, I'll be glad—"

"Captain!" Korby interrupted. His face was suddenly agitated. "I should much prefer—"

It was Kirk's turn to interrupt. He spoke loudly into the communicator. "Kirk to Rayburn. *Rayburn, are you receiving me?*"

He made an adjustment on the communicator and tried again. Then he gave himself a moment. "My other man has failed to respond, Doctor. It is now necessary that I call my ship . . ."

"No communications, Captain!"

It was Brown who had shouted. In his hand he held an old-style phaser rifle. It was aimed at Kirk's heart.

Aghast, Christine said, "Roger, what . . ."

"I'm sorry, dear," Korby said. "But if they should send down more people . . ."

Kirk, appalled by the sudden turn events had taken, realized that Andrea, rushing at him, had snatched the communicator from his hand.

"Roger!" Christine cried. "This man . . . this girl . . . Why do you allow. . . ?"

"Your captain won't be harmed," Korby said hurriedly. "Christine, listen. You must admit the possibility that there are things here unknown to you but so vitally important that—"

"Doctor Korby!" Kirk shouted. "I have one man dead! Now I've got another one out of contact!"

"Take his weapon, Andrea," Korby said.

The girl began to circle Kirk to get at the phaser hung on the rear of his belt. He drew back—and Brown leveled the rifle at his forehead. Kirk grabbed for reason. "Doctor, I have a command to consider, crewmen, a Starship . . ."

"This is necessary, Captain. You will understand."

Kirk moved. He jerked out his phaser; and all in the same blur of action, ducked behind a heavy desk.

"Drop that rifle!" he said to Brown.

Instead, Brown's finger reached for the trigger. Kirk fired his phaser—and Brown fell.

Christine screamed, "Captain, behind you . . . !"

Her warning came too late. The hairless ape-thing had him by the arm. Under the fierce force of the grip, he was lifted high into the air, his whole body convulsed by the arm's agony. The phaser rang on the stone floor. Like a puppet, he kicked, helpless in the immense hand—and the other one struck him in the jaw. Christine screamed again. And he was dropped to fall, limp, half-conscious in a crumpled heap.

Christine, paralyzed with horror, stared vaguely around her as though seeking some answer to the incomprehensible. Then she saw what she had to see. Brown lay on the floor near Kirk, face upturned. There was no blood on the chest where the phaser beam had struck him. Instead, a metallic tangle of twisted dials and wires protruded from it . . . the infinitely complex circuitry required to animate an android robot.

Kirk found the strength to move his eyes. Then, he, too, saw what Christine had seen.

An anxious Spock was at Uhura's panel when she finally received Kirk's signal.

"Frequency open, sir," she told him, relief in her face. He seized the speaker. "Spock here, Captain."

The familiar voice said, "Contact established with Doctor Korby."

"We were becoming concerned, Captain. Your check-in is overdue. Nor have we heard from your security team."

"There's no problem, Mr. Spock. They're with me. Return to ship will take about forty-eight hours. Doctor Korby's records and specimens will need careful packing."

"We can send down a work detail, sir."

"Korby has ample staff here. It's just that the work is quite delicate."

Abruptly Spock asked, "Captain . . . Is everything all right down there?"

Nothing was all right down there.

Spock had received no signal from Kirk. The captain of the *Enterprise* was sitting on a bunk in a detention chamber, watching as his voice issued from the mouth of the hairless ape-thing across the room. His communicator looked like a cigarette lighter in the creature's enormous paw. Korby was supervising its performance. He wasn't enjoying it. There was real concern for Kirk in his face. But real or unreal, Korby's feelings, his work, the man himself had ceased to matter to Kirk. The hot rage he felt had burned up all save the overriding fact that a neolithic savage was masquerading as commander of the *Enterprise.*

He tensed on the bunk. The bald thing noted it; and clicking the communicator off, prepared for muscle work.

"Please be still," Korby said. "If you move or cry out, Ruk may injure you. At least wait until you and I can talk together."

The communicator snapped back on. And a yet more anxious Spock said to Ruk, "Acknowledge, Captain. You sound tired."

Kirk heard his exact intonation come again from the flabby lips. "It's just the excitement of what we've found out, Mr. Spock. Korby's discoveries are scientifically amazing. All under control. Stand by for regular contact, Kirk out."

Ruk closed the communicator.

"This isn't a vain display, Captain," Korby said. "You know my reputation. Trust me."

"Yes, I know your reputation," Kirk said. "The whole galaxy knows who you are and what you used to stand for."

"There's so much you must learn before you make a judgment," Korby said. He turned to Ruk. "Andrea," he said tersely.

The loose mouth opened to say sweetly, "And you must be Captain Kirk of the Starship *Enterprise.*"

There was horror in the sound of the girlish voice emerging from the bald grotesque across the room. Kirk's obvious repulsion pleased it. Ruk began to show off.

It was Korby's voice now, saying, "Forgive me, Captain. It's been a long time." Then it was Christine's turn. Ruk reproduced her precise emotional inflection in the words, "I knew I'd find you."

"Enough!" Korby said sharply. "You are not to mock Christine! You are never to harm her!"

"Or disobey an order from her?" Kirk said.

Korby rose to the challenge. To Ruk he said, "You will never disobey Christine's orders." He looked at Kirk. "Satisfied, Captain?" He came over to sit beside Kirk on the bunk. Ruk rose, menacing. Korby waved him back. "Give me just twenty-four hours to convince you, Captain."

"Must I be a prisoner to be convinced?"

"What would your first duty be on return to your ship? A report! Do you realize how many vital discoveries have been lost to laymen's superstitions, their ignorance?"

"Here is an ignorant layman's question for you, Doctor," Kirk said. *"Where is my man I could not contact?"*

"Ruk is programmed to protect my experiments. The logic of his machine-mind saw danger to me . . ."

"Where is my other crewman?" Kirk repeated.

Korby's voice was very quiet. "Ruk—destroyed them

26

both, Captain. But totally against my wishes, believe me."

Kirk's fists clenched. He looked down at them; and deliberately relaxing them, swallowed. Putting interest into his voice, he said, "He's a robot, isn't he? Like Brown?"

Korby nodded to Ruk. The thing spoke heavily, dully. "More complex than Brown, much superior. The old ones made me."

Korby said, "Ruk was still tending the machinery when we arrived here. How many centuries old he is even Ruk doesn't know. With his help, with the records I could find, we built Brown."

"You've convinced me, Doctor," Kirk said. "You've convinced me that you're a very dangerous man . . ."

He pushed Korby off the bunk; and in a fast pivot, shoved him across the room at Ruk. Then he made a leap for the door. But Ruk was too quick for him. Moving with a surprising speed, the thing grabbed his arm and flung him back across the room. He struck the hard masonry of the wall, thrust against it to regain his feet—but the move was useless. He was seized and lifted, a toy in the gigantic hand.

"Careful, Ruk!" Korby shouted. "Gently!"

The vise-like grip eased. But Ruk's notion of gentleness left something to be desired. He cuffed Kirk across the head—and dropped him, unconscious.

"Where is Captain Kirk?"

Christine stopped pacing the length of Korby's study to put the question to an Andrea who'd suddenly appeared through a door. The sweetly innocent looked back at her, puzzled.

"You are concerned about the captain when you are with Roger again? I do not understand."

There was that familiar use of his name again. Christine was engulfed by a desolate sense of helplessness. She could understand nothing at all, not the man she had loved so long, his purpose nor his companions.

"Yes," she said. "I am much concerned about the captain."

With manifest sincerity, her voice wholly guileless, Andrea said, "How can you love Roger without trusting him?"

27

Christine didn't answer. The query had gone straight to the heart of her agony. She began her restless pacing again and Andrea said, "Why does it trouble you when I use the name 'Roger'?"

"It is sufficient that it does trouble her."

Korby had entered the study. Ruk was with him, the giant hand tight on Kirk's arm. The door hummed closed behind them; and Korby, moving to Andrea, said, "You will call me 'Doctor Korby' from now on."

She said, "Yes, Doctor Korby."

He took Christine's cold hand, smiling down into her eyes. "As you can see, dear, Captain Kirk is fine. He won't be harmed. What's at stake here simply makes it necessary to prevent his reporting to his ship. I need time to explain, to demonstrate to him—and to you. Shall we start with Andrea?"

"Yes," she said. "Do start with Andrea."

The girl spoke simply, openly. "I am like Doctor Brown—an android robot. You did not know?"

"Remarkable, isn't she?" Korby said. He looked back at Kirk. "Notice the lifelike pigmentation, the variation in skin tones." He lifted Andrea's wrist. "The flesh has warmth. There's even a pulse, physical sensation . . ."

"Remarkable, indeed," Christine said.

The bitter irony in her voice got through to Korby. He released Andrea's wrist. "Darling," he said to Christine, "all I require for my purpose are obedience and awareness . . ."

It was an unfortunate choice of words. Christine walked away from him. For a moment he lost his self-assurance. Then he followed her. "Christine. You must realize that an android robot is like a computer. It does only what I program into it. As a trained scientist yourself, you must surely see . . ."

". . . that given a mechanical assistant, constructing a mechanical 'geisha' would be easy?"

Korby suddenly reached for Christine, pulling her close to him. "Do you think I could love a machine?" he demanded.

"Did you?" she said.

"Love can't exist where all is predictable! Christine, you must listen! Love must have imperfection—moments

28

of worship, moments of hate. Andrea is as incapable of anger and fear as she is of love. She has no meaning for me. She simply obeys orders! Watch her . . ."

He spoke to Andrea. "Kiss Captain Kirk," he said. She kissed Kirk.

"Now strike him," Korby said.

She slapped Kirk.

"You see, Christine? All she can do is what she's told to do. She's a sterile, a computer—a thing, not a woman." He whirled to Kirk. "Have you nothing to say, Captain?"

"Yes, Doctor, I have something to say," Kirk said, "If these inventions of yours can only do what they're told to do, why did Brown attack me? Who told him to do it? For that matter, who told this thing"—he indicated Ruk—"to kill two of my men?"

Korby's face went closed, cold. Taking Christine's arm, he said, "Come with me, darling. You owe it to me." She looked at Kirk, the feeling of nightmare helplessness still heavier in her limbs. Then she went with Korby.

His laboratory was at the end of a lengthy corridor. It was spotlessly white. Cabinets of gleaming equipment shared its walls with banks of computer-like control panels. But its dominating feature was a large central turntable. It was flanked by two squat dynamos. Ruk was busy at the table. Into a scooped-out hollow in its top, he was fitting a mold of some greenish-brown stuff, roughly conformed to the height and breadth of a human body. As a cook pats dough into a bread pan, his gargantuan hands worked deftly to shape the mold into the indentation. It was when they reached for a shining, complicated mechanism suspended from the ceiling that Christine first noticed it. Then she saw there was a similar one hanging over the other side of the table. Ruk lowered the nearer device over the mold's midsection. Slowly the table began to turn.

Its opposite side slid into view. Kirk was lying on it, eyes closed, pressed down, immobile. The ceiling's other machine, descended over him, covered him from breast to thighs.

Pointing to it, Korby said proudly, "This is how we make an android robot."

With a signal to Ruk, he went over to a wall of control panels. He twisted a knob. Blue lights flashed deep, blinding, within the instrumentation that masked the alternately passing mold-form and the body of Kirk. The heavy dynamos glowed red, throbbing under impulses of power flowing to them from the control panel. When Korby made an adjustment to increase the turning speed of the table, a dizziness seized Christine. She leaned back against an equipment cabinet, her eyes shut against the vertigo. When she opened them, the blue lights were blazing, pulsating to the rhythm of a human heartbeat. And the table was spinning now, blurring the forms it held in a haze of speed so fast they appeared to be one.

Unknowingly she was wringing her hands. Korby left the panel to take them in his. "Don't be afraid for him. I promise you, he's not being harmed in any way."

She found stumbling words. "To fix a man to a table like a lab specimen on a slide . . . I don't . . . Oh, Roger, what's happened to you . . . ? I remember when I sat in your class . . ." Tears choked her. "You wouldn't even consider injuring an animal, an insect . . . Life was sacred to you . . . It was what I loved about you . . ." She was openly weeping.

He took her in his arms. "I haven't changed, Christine. This is just a harmless demonstration to convince his skeptical, military mind. Please try and understand. If I'd beamed up to his ship with Brown and the others, they would have been objects of mere curiosity, freaks—the origin of wild rumors and destructive gossip."

"You don't *know* Captain Kirk!" she cried.

He patted her shoulder. "Now is the time to watch most carefully . . ." He left her to make some new, precise adjustment on the panel. Apparently, the table had reached its maximum acceleration. It was slowing down. In mingled amazement and horror, Christine caught a glimpse of the mold-form. It had assumed detailed human shape, human skin tones. The table came to a halt before her. Its niches held two identical Kirks.

Triumphant, Korby came back to her. "Which of the two is your captain, Christine? Can you tell?"

She shook her head. "I don't . . . know. I don't know —anything any more."

"This one is your captain," Korby said. "Do you see any harm that's been done him?"

Kirk's eyes opened. Immediately aware that he couldn't move, he was struggling against the appliance that covered him when he saw Korby. His jaw muscles hardened; and he was about to speak when he decided to listen, instead. For Korby was expounding to Christine. "The android's synthetic organs are now all in place. We merely synchronized them with Kirk's autonomic nervous system, duplicating his body's rhythms. Now we must duplicate his mental patterns . . ."

A glimmer of realization came to Kirk. He saw Korby move to another control panel. He saw Andrea slip into the laboratory. And Ruk had gone into a crouch at the dynamo near his feet. He sensed what Korby was going to say before he said it. "Ruk, we're ready for final synaptic fusion. Andrea, stand by the cortex circuits. This android we're making will be so perfect, it could even replace the captain. It will have the same memories, the same abilities, the same attitudes . . ."

The implications of the boast were so appalling that they stimulated Kirk to a scurry of thinking faster than any he'd ever done in his life. As Korby shouted, *"Activate the circuits!"* he contorted his face with fury. As though mumbling to himself, he muttered, "Mind your business, Mr. Spock! I'm sick of your halfbreed interference! Do you hear me? Mind your business, Mr. Spock! I'm sick of your halfbreed—"

In midsentence a spasm of agony convulsed his body. Bolts of lightning seemed to split his head. The dynamo's hum screamed to an ear-shattering roar. Then the pain, the lightning, the roar were all over. Distraught, Christine ran to him. "I'm all right," he said. "It seems to be finished."

Korby came for her. "And now, my dear, you can meet my new android."

He gave the table a rotating twist. On it lay a perfect replica of Kirk. Its eyelids fluttered. Its gaze fastened on Christine and its lips moved in Kirk's characteristic smile of recognition. It said, "Nurse Chapel, how nice to see you."

Hostess Andrea was serving a meal to Christine in the study when Korby's new android opened its door. It was wearing Kirk's uniform.

"May I join you?" it said, seating itself at the table. "The doctor tells me I'm more or less on parole now. He thought you and I might like a little time together."

Christine whispered, "Captain, what are we . . . ?"

The android also lowered its voice. "We've got to find a way to contact the ship."

"I don't know what's happened to Roger." She looked despairingly into what she thought were Kirk's eyes.

"If I gave you a direct order to betray him, would you obey it, Christine?"

She bowed her head. "Please, Captain. Don't ask me to make such a choice. I'd rather you pushed me off the precipice where Matthews died."

Andrea placed a bowl of soup before her. "Thank you," she said. "I'm not hungry."

Her table companion also pushed its bowl aside. "I'm not, either," it said. "But then I am not your captain, Nurse Chapel. We androids don't eat, you see."

She'd thought she'd had all the shocks she could take. But there was a cat-and-mouse aspect to this last one that chilled her. She'd been about to confide her heartbreak to this manufactured thing masquerading as Kirk. She pushed her chair back and rose from the table just as Korby entered the study. The real Kirk was with him—a pale, haggard Kirk clad in the kind of nondescript lab outfit which Brown had worn.

He sniffed at the smell of food. "I'm hungry," he said; and turning to Korby, added, "That's the difference between me and your androids, Doctor."

His replica got up from its chair. "The difference is your weakness, Captain, not mine."

"Eating is a human pleasure," Kirk retorted. "Sadly, it is one you will never know."

"Perhaps. But I shall never starve, either," the android said.

Kirk looked at Korby. "It is an exact duplicate?"

"In every detail."

Kirk spoke directly to the duplicate. "Tell me about Sam, Mr. Android."

The answer came promptly. "George Samuel Kirk is your brother. Only *you* call him Sam."

"He saw me off on this mission."

"Yes. With his wife and three sons."

"He said he was being transferred to Earth Colony Two Research Station."

"No. He said he *wanted* a transfer to Earth Colony Two."

Korby intervened. "You might as well try to out-think a calculating machine, Captain."

"Obviously, I can't," Kirk said. "But we do have some interesting differences."

Korby was annoyed. "Totally unimportant ones." Abruptly, he dismissed his perfect android; and seating himself at the table, motioned Kirk and Christine to chairs. "Bring food," he told Andrea. "Lots of it. The captain is hungry."

As Kirk began eating, he leaned forward. "You haven't guessed the rest, have you? Not even you, Christine. What you saw was only a machine—*only half of what I could have accomplished had I continued the process of duplication.* I could have put *you,* Captain—your very consciousness into that android." He smiled faintly. "Your very 'soul' if you prefer the term. All of you. Brown was an example. My assistant was dying. I gave him life in android form."

Intensity came into his voice. "Yes, humans converted into androids can be programmed—but for the better! Can you conceive how life would be if we could do away with jealousy, greed, hate?"

Kirk said, "That coin has an opposite side, Doctor. You might also do away with tenderness, love, respect."

Korby slammed his fist on the table. "No death! No disease, no deformities! Even fear can be programmed out to be replaced with perpetual peace! Open your mind, Captain! I'm speaking of a practical heaven, a new Paradise—and all I need is your help!"

"I thought all you needed was my 'open mind,'" Kirk said.

"I've got to get transportation to a planet with the proper raw materials. There must be several possibilities among your next stops. I'm not suggesting any diversion from your route. I myself want no suspicion aroused. I simply want to begin producing androids more carefully, selectively . . ."

Under his chair Kirk's hand had found a thong that bound its joints together. He located one end of it. "I can see your point," he said. "Any publicity about such a project could only frighten uninformed prejudice."

Korby nodded. "My androids must be widely infiltrated into human societies before their existence is revealed. Otherwise, we'd have a tidal wave of superstitious hysteria that could destroy what is right and good. Are you with me, Captain?"

Christine was staring at Korby in unbelief. Had the years of loneliness sent him mad? To advance such a cooperation to the captain of a Federation Starship! But Kirk was taking it quietly. "You've created your own Kirk, Doctor. You don't need me."

"I created him to impress you, Captain, not to replace you."

"You'd better use him," Kirk said. "I am impressed —but not the way you intended." He had the thong unraveled now.

"Ruk!" Korby called. "Ruk, take the captain to his quarters!"

As the hairless Caliban approached him, Kirk sat still, his hand busy with a slipknot he was putting into the cord under his chair. When Ruk reached for his shoulder, he tensed for action. All in one fast move, he ducked under Ruk's arm, leaped for Korby; and, dropping the slipknot over his head, jerked it tight around his throat. Then he ran for the door. Ruk made a lunge for him but was halted by the sound of Korby's agonized choking. Turning, he saw Korby fall from his chair, hands clawing at the cord that was throttling him. He hesitated. Then he returned to Korby to loosen the noose.

Christine went to help him. But Korby, furious, pushed her away. "Get after—" he broke off, coughing. Clearing his throat, he tried again. "Get after him, Ruk. Stop him. I have no more use for him. You understand?"

Ruk understood. So did Christine. She heard the growl rumble in the great chest as Ruk made for the door. She followed him, calling, "Ruk! Ruk, stop!" She could see the huge android speeding down the lighted corridor toward what she thought were Kirk's quarters. Then the figure disappeared around a corner. She turned with it into an

34

unlighted passageway, still calling, "Ruk, stop! The doctor told you to obey my orders. Stop!"

The speed of the running footsteps increased. She raced on. "Ruk, where are you? I order you not to harm him! Do you hear me? He is not to be harmed! Ruk, where are you?"

He'd vanished into the darkness. And the character of the passage had changed. Its stone floor had become uneven and she stumbled over a pebble. It flung her against a rough, unpolished rock wall. The blackness swallowed the sound of the footsteps.

But Kirk heard them pounding behind him. He'd come to the end of the passage and was clambering over rocks. He fell into a gully between two boulders. He clung to one of them, listening.

"Captain Kirk?"

It was Ruk's voice, echoing hollowly among the rocks. Kirk hauled himself up over a boulder; and began to edge forward again through the pitch blackness, groping along a wall.

"Captain Kirk . . ."

The sound of the footsteps had ceased. But he could hear Ruk's heavy breathing, somewhere close. Frantically, Kirk felt around him for some kind of weapon. A sharp stalagmite jutted up from the floor. He wrestled with it. It was immovable. Desperate now, he seized a rock and crashed it over the stalagmite's pointed end. It broke. He scrabbled around among its pieces and found a club-like shard of it.

There came a hushed whisper. "Captain Kirk? Where are you?"

Now it was Christine's voice. Kirk peered into the darkness—and was about to answer when he remembered Ruk's trick of voice imitation.

It came again—Christine's voice. "Captain Kirk, help! I've lost my way! Don't leave me here . . ."

Was it Christine? Or was it Ruk? There was no way of telling. Kirk tightened his hold on his rock weapon. It just might be Christine, lost in this labyrinth of underground pathways. He might as well answer. The suspense was as difficult to bear as any fact would be. And he had taken all the precautions it was possible to take.

35

"Over here, Christine," he said.

Darker than the dark, the monstrous android loomed toward him, surefooted, moving easily, swiftly. Kirk struggled for solid rock under his feet, pivoted and was swinging his arm back for the strike when the edge of the rock that held him crumbled.

The solid footing he'd struggled for bordered a chasm. It fell away beneath him as sheer and deep as the one that had lost him Matthews. His fingertip clutch on its rim was his clutch on life. He fought to maintain it against the rain of stones disturbed by the crumbled edge. One struck his head. He looked up to see Ruk leaning over it. He became aware that his fingers were weakening.

More debris loosened. The rock he clawed at cracked. As it gave way, Ruk's arm snaked down to seize one of his wrists. They exchanged a long look. Then slowly Ruk hauled him back up.

Spock saw the bridge elevator open. Kirk walked out of it and turned to stride down the corridor that led to his quarters. Spock hurried after him. "Captain!" he called. "I've just received word that you had beamed up."

Kirk was at his desk, leafing through a drawer for his command orders. "Doctor Korby has considerable cargo coming aboard, Mr. Spock. I'll have to go over our destinations schedule with him."

Spock looked at the packet in his hand. Surprised, he said, "You're going back down with the command orders, sir?"

"Mind your business, Mr. Spock!" Kirk shouted savagely. "I'm sick of your halfbreed interference! Do you hear me? Mind your business, Mr. Spock! I'm sick of your halfbreed—"

Shocked, Spock stood stock-still. Kirk moved for the door. Spock, confounded, still staggered, tried again. "Are you feeling all right, Captain?"

All hardness had left Kirk's voice. He spoke quietly, his customary, courteous self. "Quite all right, thank you, Mr. Spock. I'll beam up shortly with Dr. Korby and his party." He eyed Spock, puzzled. "You look upset, Mr. Spock. Everything all right up here?"

The Vulcan looked as bewildered as he'd ever permitted himself to appear. He finally decided to compromise with a noncommittal, "No problems here, sir."

He got himself a nod, a friendly smile and Kirk's exit to the corridor. But his sense of dismayed shock persisted. He went over to the intercom button in the cabin and hit it.

"Security, this is First Officer Spock. Status of your landing party?"

"Ready and standing by, sir."

"Wait until the captain has beamed down. Then have them meet me in the Transporter Room. All of the party, the captain included."

He was asking for trouble with Kirk. On the other hand, trouble between them already existed.

Korby was pleased with his new android's performance. He shuffled through the command-orders packet and his android said, "I've looked them over. You'll find planet Midos V an excellent choice." It indicated a sheet among the others on Korby's desk.

"A small colony. And abundant raw materials." He rose. "You've made a good beginning, Captain Kirk."

"Thank you, Doctor," it said. "I felt quite at home on the *Enterprise*."

Down the corridor Kirk lay on the bed in his quarters, thinking, thinking. His life had been saved, but to what purpose he couldn't see. The *Enterprise* hijacked by the thing that wore his uniform . . . Some planet, perhaps the galaxy itself, doomed to be peopled by non-people . . . Humanoid life extinguished by the machines of Korby's making.

The door hummed open. Andrea entered with a tray of food. She placed it on the table.

Kirk sat up on his bunk. "Kiss me, Andrea," he said.

She kissed him. Then the cortical circuit that had obeyed a former order to kiss him activated the one connecting the kiss with a slap. She drew her hand back to strike him when Kirk seized it. "No," he said. He got up. Taking her in his arms, he gave her the most impassioned kiss in his repertoire. She liked it. But her circuitry protested. From somewhere in her came the tiny whine of a hard-pressed coil.

Panic-stricken, her responses chaotic, she pushed him

away, crying, "Not you . . . not programmed for you . . ."

She went weaving, half-reeling toward the door. Kirk, alarmed, followed her, only to find Ruk standing guard in the corridor.

His eyes on Kirk, Ruk said, "To maintain your life is illogical."

"Why?" Kirk said.

Ruk didn't answer. Under the hairless scalp, his brain seemed to be fighting with a swarm of thoughts that confused him more cruelly than Andrea's terrified response to the kiss. Finally, he said. "You are no longer needed here."

"You want to kill me, Ruk? Or, as Doctor Korby calls it—turn me off?"

"You cannot be programmed. You are inferior."

"I want to live," Kirk said.

"You are from the outside," Ruk said. "You make disorder here."

"I'm not programmed. But I'll do anything, no matter how illogical to stay alive. Does that disturb you, Ruk?"

"Our place was peaceful. There was no threat to existence."

"Is existence important to you, too?"

"I am programmed to exist. Therefore, I exist."

The massive face was contorted with unaccustomed thought. Kirk felt a stab of pity. He said, "Korby speaks of you as just a machine to be turned on or turned off. That is a good thing to be, is it, Ruk?"

"You are evil. Until you came all was at peace here. That was good."

"I came in peace," Kirk said. "The only difference between us is that I have emotion. I have unpredictability. And with each human, our evil unpredictability increases. How would you like to live with thousands of unpredictable humans around you, all of them evil like me?"

Ruk was staring at him. "Yes, it was so . . . long ago. I had forgotten. The old ones here, the ones who made me, they were human . . . and evil. It is still in my memory banks . . . It became necessary to destroy them."

He turned his vast bulk slowly at the sound of footsteps. White-coated, self-assured, Korby was striding down the corridor.

Ruk lumbered toward him. "You . . . *you* brought him among us," he said heavily.

Startled, Korby looked from Kirk back to Ruk. "What?"

Ruk continued to advance on him. "You brought the inferior ones here!" His voice rose. "We had cleansed ourselves of them! You brought them and their evil back!"

"Ruk, I order you to stop! Go back! Stand away from me! You are programmed to—"

It was Korby who retreated. As Ruk made a grab for him, he drew Kirk's phaser from the white coat's pocket. There was no hesitation. He fired it. Ruk was gone. Where he'd stood was a charred spot, a drift of metallic-smelling smoke.

"You didn't have to destroy him," Kirk said into the tight silence.

Korby leveled the phaser at him. "Move," he said. "Ahead of me . . ."

A tense Christine stood at the door of the study, apparently awaiting the result of Korby's visit to Kirk's quarters. At the entrance, Kirk turned to face his captor. "You were once a man with respect for all living things. How is the change in you to be explained, Doctor? If I were to tell Earth that I am your prisoner, to tell them what you have become—"

He made a grab for the phaser. But Korby used it to shove him into the study. Then the door, humming shut, caught his other hand between it and the jamb. Kirk, about to exploit his advantage, paused. Korby's wedged hand was being cruelly mashed. Yet his right hand still held the phaser in an unwavering aim at Kirk. It seemed a remarkable fortitude. When he wrenched the smashed hand free, it struck Kirk as yet more remarkable.

Then a slow horror chilled him. Christine, too, was staring at the injured hand. Instead of revealing torn and mangled flesh, the wound had exposed a fine mesh of tiny complex gears and pulsing wires. Some connection in the wires short-circuited. A wisp of smoke rose from it, leaving a smell of scorched metal.

Korby saw Christine's face. "It's still me, Christine—your Roger . . . in this android form . . . You can't imagine why—how it was with me. I was frozen, dying, my legs were gone. I had only my brain between death and life . . ." He lifted the hand. "This can be repaired, more easily than any surgeon could possibly repair it. I'm the same man that you knew and loved—a better one. There will never be any death for me . . . never . . ."

She put her hands over her face to shut out the sight of the dangle of still-pulsing wires. Korby, turning to Kirk, cried, "Imagine it, Captain! A world with no corruption, no suffering, no death . . ."

"Then why keep me alive, Doctor?" Kirk said. "I am mere flesh and blood. So I shall die. You've got yourself an immortal Kirk. Why don't you kill this mortal one—and get done with me?"

"You know that answer," Korby said. "I am still the man you described—the one with respect for all living things. I am still that man."

"You are not that man, Doctor," Kirk said. "Look at Christine . . . heartbroken, terrified. Where is your human response to her suffering?"

As the question was taken in by his computer brain, Korby looked shaken. Its whirring circuits churned to no effective answer. So it dismissed the question. Recovering his composure, he went to a speaker built into a wall. "Andrea," he said, "come to the study."

The door hummed open and Kirk laid his arm around Christine's shoulders.

"Yes, Doctor," Andrea said.

"Someone is coming down the corridor," Korby told her.

"I will find Ruk," she said.

"Ruk has been turned off. Get Brown's weapon! Fast! Deal with it. *Protect!*"

She found Brown's old-style phaser in a desk drawer and hurried out of the study.

In full uniform, Kirk's facsimile was sauntering along the corridor. Its appearance puzzled Andrea. It also interested her. She moved toward the android, lifting her face to it.

"I will kiss you," she said.

"No!" it said sharply.

A look of anger flickered over her face.

40

"Protect," she said. Then she pulled the trigger of the phaser rifle. She looked down at the black ash that was all that remained, sniffing curiously at the drift of smoke. "Protect," she said again—and returned to the study.

Korby was shouting wildly. "I'm the *same!* A direct transfer—*all of me!* Wholly rational . . . human but without a flaw!"

Smiling, innocent, Andrea said, "I just turned off Captain Kirk."

"She's killed your perfect android," Kirk said. "Just as you killed Ruk. Is this your perfect world? Your flawless beings? Killing, killing, killing! Aren't you flawless beings doing exactly what you most hate in humans? Killing with no more feeling than you feel when you turn off a light?"

This time the computer brain was unable to dismiss the question. Kirk extended his hand. "Give me that phaser, Doctor. If any of the human Korby remains in you, you must know that your only hope is to give me that gun."

"No! You refuse to understand! I have constructed perfect beings . . . tested them . . ." Korby's face seemed to shrivel as his brain circuits told him he'd contradicted himself. His own illogic got through to them. "I—I have proven they are perfect . . . I . . . I have . . ."

With a look of blank bafflement, he gave the phaser to Kirk. Pale as death, Christine sank down on a chair.

"Give me your rifle, Andrea," Kirk said.

"No," she said. She waved him back with the weapon. "No . . . protect . . ." She moved to Korby. "I am programmed to love you, protect you. To kiss you . . ." She lifted her face to his.

Christine moaned faintly. Stunned, she watched Korby push Andrea away. "Don't touch me," he said. "You cannot love, you machine!" But Andrea still clung to him. The phaser she held came into position between them as Korby fought to free himself from her arms. "Programmed," Andrea said. "To love you . . . to kiss you . . ."

The rifle discharged. There was a flash of light. Then that, too, was gone. All that was left was the blur of smoke, the two piles of ash on the floor.

Dry-eyed, stumbling, Christine moved to Kirk. She was shuddering uncontrollably. He held her, the heiress to a permanent legacy of disillusioned loneliness.

As the last of the smoke dissolved, the study door was wrenched open. Spock and two security crewmen, phasers drawn, entered the study.

"Captain . . ." Spock hesitated. "You're all right, sir? Nurse Chapel?"

"All right, Mr. Spock," Kirk said.

"Where is Dr. Korby?" Spock asked.

Kirk took Christine's hand. "He was never here, Mr. Spock."

He took it again when she approached his command chair in the bridge of the *Enterprise*.

"Thank you for letting me make my decision, Captain," she said. "I'm fairly certain I'm doing the right thing."

"I am, too," he said. "Maybe you can get some sleep now that your decision is made."

Neither smiled. "I'll be seeing you around," she said.

When she'd left the bridge, Spock said, "She's brave."

"That's why we need her on the *Enterprise*, Mr. Spock." He looked at the viewing screen. "Helm, steady as she goes. Nurse Chapel has decided to remain with us." But Spock still stood at the command chair. "Something bothering you, Mr. Spock?"

"Captain, I . . . must protest your using the term 'halfbreed' in reference to me."

"I didn't *use* it, Mr. Spock. I directed it toward you as a—"

"Even as an android, you might have thought of a better expression," Spock said.

Kirk eyed him gravely. "I'll remember that, Mr. Spock, when I find myself in a similar position again."

"Thank you, sir," Spock said.

The Squire of Gothos

(Paul Schneider)

The planet had given no hint of its existence to the *Enterprise*. Uncharted, unsuspected, undetected, it finally confessed its presence to the Starship's sensors. At Spock's sudden announcement of their new reading, Kirk in some annoyance flipped a switch—and sure enough, out of what should have continued to be the empty, star-void quadrant of space they were traversing, a crescent-shaped body swam into abrupt, unusually brilliant, magnified focus on the bridge viewing screen.

Kirk glared at it. It was an unwelcome distraction from his job—a mission to get needed supplies to Colony Beta 6; and get them there by an uninterrupted warp factor three speed across this apparent space desert, barren of stars. He spoke tersely. "Navigation report."

Crewman De Salle looked up from his computations. "Iron-silicate substance, Captain, planet-sized magnitude One-E. We'll be passing close."

The puzzled Spock had left his station to come and stand by the command chair. Eyes on the screen, he said, "It is incredible that this body has gone unrecorded on all our charts, sir."

So, Kirk thought, imagination must bestir itself,

stretching the credible to include the incredible. There was a certain dryness in his retort. "But there it is, Mr. Spock, incredible though it be." He swung around to face his bridge people. "We can't stop to investigate now. All science stations will gather data for computer banks. Lieutenant Uhura, report the discovery of this planet on subspace radio."

She struggled to obey the order. Then she turned. "Strong interference on subspace, sir. The planet must be a natural radio source."

"Then let's get out of its range," Kirk said. He twisted his chair around to the helm console. "Veer off forty degrees, Mr. Sulu."

As Sulu reached for a control on his board, he disappeared. One moment he was there, substantial, familiar, intently competent—and the next, his chair was as empty as though vacancy had always been its appointed function. "*Sulu!*" Kirk shouted, leaping for the helm. Then he, too, was gone, vanished as utterly as Sulu. Navigator De Salle, taut-faced, sprang from his station. "They're *gone,* Mr. Spock! *They're both gone!*"

Spock, at the abandoned command console, twisted a dial. Obediently, alarm sirens shrieked through the ship. It was the beginning of a general, deck-to-deck scrutiny of its every nook and cranny. As Spock dismissed the last discouraged search party, he turned to the big, blond meteorologist beside him. "They're either down on that planet—or nowhere." Overhearing, De Salle said tensely, "But there's still no sign of human life on the surface, sir. Of course the probe instruments may be malfunctioning."

Spock eyed his board. "They are functioning normally," he said. "Continue sensor sweeps. Lieutenant Uhura, have you covered all wave-bands?"

"All of them, sir. No response."

De Salle was on his feet. "With due respect, sir, I request permission to transport down to the surface to carry the search on there!"

McCoy had joined the group at the command chair. Now he grabbed Spock's arm. "I agree! What are we waiting for, Spock?"

"The decision will be mine, Doctor. I hold the responsibility for your safety." Blandly ignoring McCoy's out-

44

raged glare, he addressed the big meteorologist. "Dr. Jaeger, please describe your geophysical findings on the surface below."

"No detectable soil or vegetation . . . extremely hot. The atmosphere is toxic, swept by tornadic storms . . . continuous volcanic activity . . . inimical to any life as we know it, without oxygen life support."

"How would you estimate the survival time of two unprotected men down there?"

"As long as it would take to draw one breath."

Nobody spoke. Then Uhura broke the heavy stillness. "Mr. Spock! My viewing screen! Look!" All eyes on the bridge veered to her station. There on the screen, letters—letters formed in flowing, old-English script—had begun to appear. Gradually they extended themselves until the message they were intended to convey had completed itself. Astoundingly out of tune with the somber mood of the bridge people, it was: "Greetings and felicitations."

Spock read it aloud without inflection. "Greetings . . . and . . . felicitations. Send this, Lieutenant. U.S.S. *Enterprise* to signaler on planet surface. Identify yourself. We—" He broke off as more letters assembled themselves into words on the screen. After a moment, he read them aloud, too, slowly, unbelievingly. "Hip . . . hip . . . hurrah," he said, "and I believe that last word is pronounced 'tallyho'?"

"Some kind of joke, sir?" De Salle said.

Spock glanced at him. "I shall entertain any theories, Mr. De Salle. Any at all . . ."

McCoy spoke up. "One thing is certain. There *is* life on that planet!"

"You would seem to be correct, Doctor," Spock said. He reached for the intercom; and had just ordered preparation of the Transporter Room when Scott, pushing his way toward him, reached him and said, "Request assignment to the search party, sir."

Sometimes Spock's eyes seemed to be looking at one from a great distance. They had that faraway look in them now as he shook his head. "No, Mr. Scott. Neither you nor I can be spared here. Mr. De Salle, you will equip landing party with full armaments, with life support and communication gear. Doctor Jaeger, your geophysical knowledge

45

may be crucial. Doctor McCoy will accompany, too. If those peculiar signals come from Captain Kirk and Sulu, their rationality is in question."

He waited to issue his final order until the landing group had taken position on the Transporter Platform's indentations. Then, handing De Salle a black box, he said, "Once on the surface, you will establish immediate contact with us—and by this laser beam, if necessary."

Scott worked his switches. And the three figures began their dissolution into shining fragments.

They hadn't precisely formulated what they had expected. A kind of murderous combine of earth tremors, buffetings by hurricane whirlwinds, the suffocating heat of a planet torn by cosmic forces at war below the fissured lava of its tormented surface, the coughing inhalation of lung-searing gases. But what they found differed from their vaguely shaped apprenhensions. It was a forest, cool, green, its leafy aisles tranquil, shadowy. Around the boles of its trees, flowering vines circled, scenting the fresh air with their blossoms' fragrance. Dumbfounded, McCoy watched a leaf flutter down from the bough over his head.

His voice was thick through his life-support filter. "Jaeger, where are your storms?"

Shaking his head, the meteorologist checked the instrument he held. "An atmosphere, McCoy—exactly the same as our own!"

Remembering, De Salle, removing his face mask, cried, "Ship communication and report!" But something was wrong with his communicator—a contagious wrongness that affected all their communicators. De Salle didn't give up. As he pointed the laser beam skyward, he said, "Keep trying . . . keep trying." Then he frowned. "Something's blocking this beacon. Got to find open ground . . ."

Backing off, he rounded a clump of bush. And halted, noting the reflection of flickering light on its dark leaves. Very slowly he turned. He was face to face with a stone griffin. Its wings were lifted high over the glaring features of its lion's visage. In one outstretched talon, it held a flaming torch.

"Dr. McCoy! Dr. Jaeger! Over here!"

There were two griffins, both holding torches. It was McCoy who first spotted the dark, massive, iron-bound

46

door flanked by its guardian beasts of heraldry. The door was ajar. De Salle, moving into the lead, unlimbered his phaser. Followed by the others, he pushed through the half-open entry. Except for the crackling of what looked like a big hearth fire, absolute stillness greeted them.

"In the name of heaven . . . where are we?" McCoy muttered.

Where they were was in a spacious Victorian drawing room, chandelier-lit. The wall over the burning logs of its fireplace held an arrangement of crossed swords, muskets, pistols and battle flags. Its other walls were hung with tapestries, with portraits of ancestors in armor, in the colorful uniforms of the Napoleonic wars. Near a gleaming mahogany table, a sideboard glittered with gold dishes. A harpsichord stood under a curved, gilt-framed mirror. All was in order. Everything fitted into the picture of a benevolently self-indulgent Victorianism. Except for one thing. Certain niches pressed into the urbane walls revealed a peculiar taste in statuary. They held carved shapes of lizard-like creatures, tortured-looking dolphins, a pair of giant, humanoid forms—and a tentacled spider-thing.

Suddenly, De Salle shouted: *"Look!"*

At the end of the room was an inset, a hollow gouged prominently out of its wall. As the other niches held statuary, this one held the stiffened forms of Kirk and Sulu, their attitudes caught and hardened as they had last moved at the instant before their disappearance. Their figures were bathed in a violet light. De Salle rushed to them, calling, "Dr. McCoy—quick! Dr. McCoy!"

But McCoy's health monitor was grimly factual. He looked up from it, his face tired-looking. "Nothing," he said. "Kirk and Sulu . . . like waxwork shapes . . ."

The drawing room's door slammed shut. A moment later, a tinkling Mozart-like arpeggio came from the harpsichord. And seated on the bench before it was the player —a man, a man clad in the silver-buckled elegance of a military man of the mid-1800's—a delighted if slightly sly smile on his rosy face.

As the *Enterprise* trio stared at him, he completed the musical passage with a flourish of well-groomed hands. Then he spun around to face them. He was Byronically handsome, from his pouting mouth and neckcloth-length hair to his disdainful air of superiority, of being set apart as an object of special and peculiar value and privilege. The gesture he made toward the hollow holding the forms of Kirk and Sulu was either genuinely bored—or the blossom of a painstaking cultivation of boredom.

"I must say," the musician said amiably, "that they make an exquisite display pair." Then a note of regret drooped the voice. "But I suppose you'll want them back now."

A lace-cuffed hand was lifted. Instantly, Kirk started forward, completing his interrupted move to the helm of the *Enterprise*. Sulu stirred, his face confused, his eyes bewildered. They sought Kirk's face. "Captain, where are we?"

The man on the harpsichord bench rose. "Welcome to my island of peace on this stormy little planet of Gothos."

Kirk ignored him to speak to his men. "What's happened? Fill me in."

McCoy said, "Jim, you disappeared from the bridge after Sulu went. We've been hunting you for hours—"

Their host cut across him. "You must excuse my whimsical way of fetching you here. But when I saw you passing by, I simply could not resist entertaining you."

Kirk, exchanging a glance with McCoy, stepped forward. "I am Captain James Kirk of the United Starship *Enterprise . . .*"

The creature swept him a bow. "So you are the captain of these brave men! My greetings and felicitations, Captain. It's so good of you and your officers to drop in. Absolutely smashing of you!"

The theatricality of the voice and gesture was as turgid as old greasepaint. Kirk had to make an effort to keep his voice level. "Who are you?" he said. "Where do you come from?"

An arm swept wide in a grandly embracing movement. "Have no fear, lads," said the too-rich voice. "I have made myself as one of you . . ."

De Salle's temper, compounded of fear mingled with rage, exploded. He advanced, his phaser on aim. "Who are you? That is the question that was asked you! Answer it! And make the answer fast!"

The being appreciated De Salle. "Ah, such spirited ferocity!" it crowed happily. Then, not unlike a child remembering lessons in manners, it said, "Oh, forgive me. General Trelane, retired. At your service, gentlemen. My home is your home."

It failed to soothe De Salle's temper. Low-voiced, he spoke to Kirk. "Captain, we've lost contact with the ship. We're trapped here."

Overhearing, General Trelane rubbed his hands in exuberant pleasure. " 'Trapped here,' " he echoed. "I cannot tell you how it delights me—having visitors to this very planet I have made my hobby. From my observations I did not think you capable of such voyages."

Jaeger, whispering to Kirk, gestured around them. "Captain, note the period—nine hundred light-years from Earth. This place and time fit what might have been seen if there were telescopes powerful enough to—"

He was stopped by the smile on Trelane's full red lips. "Yes. I have been an interested witness of your lively little doings on your lively little Earth, sir . . ."

"Then you've been witnessing its doings of nine hundred years past," Kirk said. "That's a long time."

Trelane chuckled. "Good heavens, have I made a time error? How fallible of me!" Eyeing the stately room around him, he added, "I did so want to make you feel at home. In fact, I am quite proud of the detail."

"General Trelane—" Kirk began; and stopped at the coyly cautionary finger that had been held up. "Tut-tut, a retired general, sir. Just Squire Trelane, now. You may call me 'Squire'—indeed, I rather fancy the title."

In his career as a Starship captain, Kirk had encountered many oddments of galactic creation—oddments ranging from the ultimately hideous and alien, to a beauty that spoke with the final familiarity of wonder to the soul. At this moment, face to face with this self-styled squire of a self-chosen time of a Victorian England, chosen out of all the times offered by nine hundred years, he seemed to be face to face with the last anomaly—an X of mystery compounded simultaneously of innocence and guile. He looked at Squire Trelane. "For what purpose have you imprisoned us here?" he asked.

Even as he spoke, he had the sense of spider-strands, sticky, well-woven, encompassing him. It was as though he had already heard what the too-rich voice was saying. "Imprisoned? Nonsense! You are my guests." His host's lower lip actually trembled with what suggested itself as the touching eagerness of hospitality. "You see, I was just completing my studies of your curious and fascinating society. You happened by at a most propitious moment." There was a low, carved, armless chair beside him and he flung himself into it. "Captain Kirk, you must tell me all about your campaigns—your battles—your missions of conquest . . ."

For the first time, Kirk seemed to know where he was. For the first time since Sulu's disappearance from the *Enterprise,* he felt a sense of firm identity, of some unnamable stability back under his feet. "Our missions are peaceful," he said. "They are not for conquest. We battle only when we have no choice."

Trelane winked at him. His left eyelid dropped and rose in inescapable suggestion of mutual, known, if unacknowledged awareness of perfidious doings in high places. "So that's the official story, eh, Captain?"

Unobtrusively, McCoy had directed his tricorder at Trelane. Just as unobtrusively, Kirk had registered this fact. Now he stepped toward the low, armless chair. "Squire Trelane," he said, "I must ask you to let us return to our ship."

What he got was a languid wave of a languid hand. "Wouldn't hear of it!" Trelane protested. "You will all join me in a repast. There is so much I must learn from you: you *feelings* about war . . . about killing . . . about conquest—that sort of thing." A finger of the languid hand became unlanguid. It stiffened, pointed, aiming at Kirk. "You are, you know," said Trelane, "one of the new predator species—species that preys even on itself."

De Salle, beside Kirk, seemed to go suddenly thick in the neck. His hand darted to his phaser. "Sir?" he said, half in question, half in appeal.

"On 'stun,' De Salle," Kirk said. "Don't kill him."

What was it about this being that both repelled and at the same time broke your heart? A capacity for communicating loneliness, that burden of the solitary self borne either in a conscious fortitude or in a necessity of unaware resentment and complaint? It was speaking, the strange

50

being. "De Salle—is that his name, Captain Kirk?" In its eagerness it didn't wait for an answer but rushed on, crying to the navigator, *"Vous êtes un vrai français?"*

"My ancestry is French . . . Yes . . ."

"Ah, *monsieur! Vive la gloire! Vive Napoleon!* I admire your Napoleon very much, y'know."

"Mr. De Salle is our navigator," Kirk said evenly. "This gentleman is our medical officer, Dr. McCoy—our helmsman, Sulu, and our meteorologist, Carl Jaeger . . ."

Trelane acknowledged each introduction. "Welcome, good physicianer. All reverence to your ancestors, Honorable Sir . . ."

Sulu flushed. "What's he doing—kidding?"

But Trelane's interest had fixed on Jaeger. Clicking his heels, he cried, *"Und Offizier Jaeger, die deutsche Soldat, nein?"* Then stamping his feet in cadence to his words, he declaimed, *"Eins, zwei, drei, vier! Gehen wir mit dem Schiessgewehr!"*

Jaeger's voice was dry as dead bone. "I am a scientist —not a military man."

Trelane beamed at him. "Come now, we are all military men under the skin. And how we do love our uniforms!" He clearly loved his—and the sight of himself in it, epauletted, be-braided as the gilt-framed mirror that reflected it back to him flushed his face with self-admiring pride. He turned, preening to get a three-quarter view of his cuirass of shining buttons; and Kirk, under his breath, spoke to De Salle. *"Now!"* But as the phaser lifted to aim, Trelane wheeled, lifting his hand. At once, De Salle stiffened into immobility.

"What is that interesting weapon you have there?" inquired the Squire of Gothos. He removed the phaser—and thaw replaced the frozen stillness of De Salle's figure. "Ah, yes, I see! That won't kill—but this will! The mechanism is now clear to me." Making an adjustment, he fired the phaser at the niche contaning the lizard-like sculpture. It dematerialized. Trelane laughed with delight. "Oh, how marvelous!" Swinging the weapon around, he shot at all the statues set in their niches around the room, yelling as each disintegrated and vanished. "Devastating!" howled Trelane. "Why this could kill millions."

Striding up to him, Kirk tore the phaser from his hand. "Beginning with whom, Trelane? My crew? Are we your next targets?"

The full red lips pouted. "But how absolutely typical of your species, Captain! You don't understand, so you're angry." He pointed a gleeful finger at Kirk. "But do not be impatient. I have anticipated your next wish. You wish to know how I've managed all this, don't you?"

He nodded in answer to his own question. Then, weaving his fingers together like a prissy English schoolmaster about to dissertate on Virgil's prosody, he said, "We —meaning others and myself—have, to state the matter briefly, perfected a system by which matter can be changed to energy . . . and then back to matter . . ."

"Like the Transporter system aboard the *Enterprise*," Kirk said.

"Oh, that's a crude example! Ours is an infinitely more sophisticated process. You see, we not only transport matter from place to place but we can alter its shape, too, at will."

"This drawing room then," Kirk said. "You created it? By rearranging the existing matter of the planet?"

"Quite," Trelane said.

"But how—"

The creature drew a soothing finger across a furrow of irritation that had appeared on its brow. "Dear Captain, your inquiries are becoming tiresome. Why? I want you to be happy—to free your mind of care. Let us enjoy ourselves in the spirit of martial good fellowship!"

Kirk turned quietly to his men. "Let's go. We're getting out of here."

"Naughty captain!" Trelane said. "Fie, you are quite rude. But you cannot leave here. What an admirably fiery look of protest! Upon my soul, I admire you, sir, though in mercy you seem to need another demonstration of my authority—"

His right hand made a swift gesture; and where Kirk had stood was emptiness. Then he was back—but on his knees, racked by choking paroxysms of agony. Dismissed from the shelter of Trelane's domain, he had been exposed to the blasting effects of the planet's lethal atmosphere. In a moment its toxic gases had licked into his lungs. He coughed, doubled over, still tortured by their strangulating vapors—and the Squire of Gothos patted his bent head.

"That was an example," he said, "of what can occur away from my kindly influence. I do hope that you will now behave yourself, Captain, not only for your own sake, but because, if you don't, I shall be very angry."

Power. It had nothing to do with morality, with responsibility. Like Trelane's, it simply existed—a fact to which the body was obliged to bow but which the heart could continue to reject, to despise.

"Let me hold on," Kirk thought.

The sensors of the *Enterprise* had finally located Trelane's cool green oasis. Scott, staring at its tranquil trees on the bridge viewing screen, said, "An area as peaceful as Earth. But how do you explain it, Mr. Spock?"

"I don't, Mr. Scott. It just is. Artificial, perhaps—a freak of nature. But the fact remains that life could exist in that space. See if you can tune the sensors down finer. See if you can pick up any sentient life forms in that area of Gothos."

As Scott moved to obey, he said, "Even if we find any, it doesn't follow that it would be our people, sir."

"No. But if the captain is alive and down there, *he has to be there in that place.* I shall try to transport up any thinking beings our sensors detect."

"Shootin' in the dark, Mr. Spock."

The retort was unanswerable. "Would you rather stand by and do nothing?"

At the same moment, in the drawing room of Trelane Hall, Kirk and his men were being herded past a cabinet. "And in here," its owner was boasting, "is an array of your battle flags and pennants, some dating back to the Crusades, to Hannibal's invaders, the hordes of Persia!"

Nobody looked at the display. Undaunted, the enthusiastic Trelane addressed Kirk. "Can you imagine it, Captain? The thousands—no, the millions—who have marched off to death singing beneath these banners! Doesn't it make your blood run swiftly to think of it?" In his exuberance, he rushed to the harpsichord to bang out some martial music. Under the cover of its noise, Sulu whispered, "Captain, where could he possibly come from? Who is this maniac?"

McCoy, his voice lowered, said, "Better ask 'what' is he. I monitored him. What I found was unbelievable."

Kirk was staring intently at the musician. Now he spoke, anticipating McCoy's news. "He's not alive."

"No, Jim. Not as we define life. No trace. Zero."

"You mean, your readings show he's dead?" Sulu asked.

"They don't even show that he exists, either alive or dead."

Jaeger pointed to the fireplace. "Notice that wood fire, Captain. Burning steadily—ember-bed red and glowing—yet it gives off no heat at all."

Kirk, moving quietly the length of the room, opened his communicator. Briefly, his voice toneless, he brought Spock up-to-date on the current situation.

"Fire without heat," Spock echoed reflectively. "It would seem, Captain, that the being mistakes all these things it has created for manifestations of present-day Earth. Apparently, it is oblivious of the time differential."

"Yes, Mr. Spock. Whatever it is we are dealing with, it is certainly not all-knowledgeable. He makes mistakes."

"And strangely simple ones. He has a flaw, sir."

"We'll work on it, Mr. Spock. Kirk out." As he snapped off his communicator, he realized that the music had stopped; and that Trelane, turning, was smiling at him. It was a sly smile, its slyness at variance with the joviality of his tone. "Discussing deep-laid plans, I'll wager. Captain, I can't wait to see them unfold."

Kirk took a firm step forward. "Trelane, I haven't planned any—"

A reproving finger was coyly waggled at him. "Ah, you mustn't believe that I deplore your martial virtues of deception and stratagem! Quite the contrary—I have nothing but esteem for your whole species!"

"If your esteem is genuine"—Kirk paused to draw a deep breath—"then you must respect our sense of duty, too. Our ship is in need of us—we have tasks to perform—schedules to honor . . ."

"Oh, but I can't bear to let you go. I was getting a bit bored until you came." He whirled on his bench to run off a bragging cadenza on the harpsichord. "You'll have to stay. I insist."

"For how long?"

"Until it's over, of course," Trelane said.

"Until what's over?"

Trelane shrugged. "Dear Captain, so many questions . . . Why worry about an inevitably uncertain future? Enjoy yourself today, my good sir. Tomorrow—why, it may never come at all. Indeed, when it arrives, it has already become today."

The phrase "slippery as an eel" suddenly occurred to Kirk. He made another try. "Trelane, even if we wanted to stay, our companions are missing us. They need us."

"I must try to experience your sense of concern with you, your grief at the separation." The harpsichord wailed a mournful minor passage, sentimental, drippy.

Kirk gritted his teeth. "There are four hundred men and women on board our ship waiting for—"

"Women!" A discordant chord crashed from the instrument. "You don't actually mean members of the fair sex are among your crew! How charming! No doubt they are very beautiful!" Trelane, leaping to his feet, clapped his hands. "And I shall be so very gallant to them! Here, let me fetch them down to us at once!"

He had lifted his arm when Kirk jumped forward. "Absolutely not!"

"No?"

"*No!*" Kirk shouted. "This game has gone far enough. Our feminine crew members are crucial operating personnel! You can't just remove them from—"

Trelane stamped his foot. "I can do anything I like! I thought you would have realized that by now!"

McCoy spoke. "Jim! I am receiving a Transporter signal!"

Trelane started wringing his hands. "What does he mean? You must tell me!"

"It means the party's over, thanks to Mr. Spock! That's what it means, Trelane"—and Kirk, signaling to his men, assumed the Transporting stance. As the others followed suit, Trelane hurried up to them. "Wait!" he screamed. "What are you doing? I haven't dismissed you. Stop! I won't have this!"

The drawing room, the florid, furious face disappeared; and this time it was Spock who hurried up to them as they shimmered into full shape on the Transporter platform.

"Captain! Are you all right?"

Kirk stepped off the platform. "Report, Mr. Spock. How were the scanners able to penetrate that radiation field?"

"They didn't, sir. Not clearly. We merely beamed up all the life forms within a given space."

McCoy broke in. "Jim, that confirms what I said. Trelane is not a life form as we know it—or he'd be coming through the Transporter now."

Kirk nodded. Then he snapped out orders. "Prepare to warp out at once! Maximum speed! Everyone to stations!"

In the bridge, the substitute personnel quickly resigned their posts to Sulu and De Salle. The pretty yeoman on duty rushed up to Kirk. "Oh, Captain," cried Teresa Ross, "we were all so worried about you!" What she meant was, "*I* was worried about you, James Kirk"—and Kirk, gravely acknowledging her concern, said, "Thank you, Yeoman Ross." Then he was on the intercom. "Scotty! I want every ounce of power your engines have. We're going to put a hundred million miles between us and that madman down there."

"Aye, sir. Welcome back, Captain."

McCoy was staring at the hand he had extended. "I'm quaking," he said. "Jim, I'm quaking—but I don't know if it's with laughter or with terror!"

Uhura looked away from her board, her eyes bright with curiosity. "What was it? What's down there on Gothos?" she asked.

"Something I hope I forget to tell my grandchildren about . . ."

Then McCoy noted the astounded expression on Teresa's face. "Look—!" she whispered. Spock had jumped to his feet, staring.

Across the bridge in the angle made by its wall and elevator shaft, Trelane stood. He was uniformed, resplendent, a sabre scabbard attached to his cummerbund. His hands were clasped behind his back and he was looking the *Enterprise* bridge over. After a moment, he spoke. "But where are all the weapons? Don't you display your weapons?"

Kirk rose slowly to his feet. Trelane made a benevolently reassuring gesture. "Don't fret, Captain. I'm only a little upset with you." He was glancing around at the bridge people.

He said, "This Mr. Spock you mentioned—the one responsible for the imprudent act of taking you from me. Which is he, Captain?"

Spock said, "I am Mr. Spock."

"Surely," said Trelane, "you are not an *officer*." He turned in amazement—real or feigned, who could know? —to Kirk. "He isn't quite human, is he?"

"My father," Spock said, "is from the planet Vulcan."

"Are its natives predatory?"

"Not specifically," Spock said solemnly.

Trelane made a dismissing gesture. "No. I should think not." He made an elaboration of turning to Kirk. "You *will* see to his punishment?"

"On the contrary," Kirk said. "I commend his action."

The full red lips pursed in their habitual pout. "But I don't like him."

Kirk won his battle for control. Tonelessly, he said, "Trelane, get off my ship! I've had enough of you!"

"Nonsense, Captain. You're all coming back with me."

The victory for control was abruptly lost. There was an obscenity about Trelane's middle-aged willfulness. Flaring, Kirk yelled, "We're not going anywhere! This ship is leaving here whether you—"

"Fiddle-de-dee," Trelane retorted. "I have a perfectly enchanting sojourn on Gothos planned for you. And I won't have you spoil it."

In a kind of prophetic awareness, Kirk knew what Trelane would do. He did it. Saying, "The decor of my draw-

57

ing room is much more appropriate . . ." He raised his arm.

And the *Enterprise* bridge was replaced by the drawing room. All that was different were the positions of the bridge people. De Salle and Sulu were seated at a dining table, laden with dishes of unidentifiable but delicious-looking foods. Uhura found herself on the bench before the harpsichord. And Trelane, completing the sentence spoken on the *Enterprise*, said, "And much more tasteful, don't you think?"

Sulu looked at the wall niches emptied of their sculptures.

"No," he said.

Trelane gave him an Oriental bow from the waist. "Yes, it is so much more fitting, Honorable Guest." He paused, catching a mirrored glimpse of his well-padded calves in their leg-hose; and the fatuous look of self-admiration on his face exploded the last remnants of De Salle's control.

"You little——!" he snarled and charged Trelane.

Kirk cried out a warning but it came too late. Trelane had made his hand wave—and once again, De Salle went stiff, immovable. Interestedly, Trelane circled him, peering into his frozen face. "Ah, what primitive fury! He is the very soul of sublime savagery!"

Kirk said, "Trelane, let him go." He repeated the sentence. *"I said, 'Let him go!'"*

Trelane stared at him. Then he nodded. "Yes, of course. I forget I must not frighten you too much. But then, you must not provoke me again. For your own sake, I warn you. I am sometimes quite short-tempered." There came another slight move of his hand; and De Salle relaxed the hands that had been reaching for Trelane's throat. Kirk clamped a firm hold on him. Sulu, seizing his other arm, whispered harshly, "De Salle, we don't even have our phasers!"

"Come, everyone!" Trelane, over at the table, pointed to chairs. "Let us forget your bad manners! Let us be full of merry talk and sallies of wit! See, here are victuals to delight the palate and brave company to delight the mind!" Pouring brandy, he offered glasses to McCoy and Sulu. "Partake, good Doctor. And you, Honorable Guest, you likee, too." Then it was the turns of De Salle and Jaeger. *"Allons, enfants! Zum Kampf, mein Herr!"*

His men looked tensely at Kirk. Nodding at the table, he said, "Play along. That's an order!"

As they began to pick halfheartedly at the lavish array of food, Kirk, Spock beside him, was giving Trelane a look of deep concentration. What was the secret of his power? Vain, silly, a showoff and braggart, he yet possessed the secret that had enabled him to establish a habitable enclave on an uninhabitable planet and to do what he said he could do—transport matter at will. In the florid face and features, there was no indication of the acute intelligence required to evolve his tricks. In fact, his look of fatuity was more pronounced than ever as, turning to Kirk, he said, "I fear you àre derelict in your social duty, Captain. You have not yet introduced me to the charming contingent of your crew."

There was a small silence before Kirk spoke to Uhura and Teresa. "This is—General Trelane."

"Retired," Trelane corrected him. "However, if you prefer, dear ladies, you may address me simply as the lonely Squire of Gothos."

Still introducing, Kirk said, "This lady is Uhura, our communications officer . . ."

Trelane went to her, took her hand and bowed over it. "A Nubian prize, eh, Captain? Taken no doubt in one of your raids of conquest. She has the same melting eyes of the Queen of Sheba . . . the same lovely skin color . . ."

With a poorly disguised shudder, Uhura pulled her hand free; and unfazed, brashly melodramatic as ever, Trelane turned to Teresa. "And this lady?" Hand over heart, he burst into recitation.

> "Is this the face that launched a thousand ships
> And burnt the topless towers of Ilium?
> Fair Helen, make me immortal with a kiss!"

Teresa flushed, stepping back; and Kirk, to distract Trelane's unwelcome attention from her, went on quickly. "Yeoman Teresa Ross. You've met Mr. Spock, our Science Officer." Trelane looked Spock up and down. "You realize," he said, "it is only in deference to the Captain that I brought you down?"

"Affirmative," Spock said.

"I don't think I like your tone. It's most challenging. Is that what you're doing—challenging me?"

"I *object* to you," Spock said. "I object to intellect without discipline; to power without purpose."

"Why, Mr. Spock," cried Trelane, "you *do* have a saving grace! You're ill mannered . . . the human half of you, no doubt. But I am wasting time . . ." He grabbed Teresa's hands. "Come, my wood nymph! Dance with your swain! And you, dear Nubian beauty, give us some sprightly music!"

"I do not know how to play this instrument," Uhura said.

"Of course you do!"

Uhura looked at Kirk. Then, turning, she fingered the harpsichord keyboard; and was startled to hear the rush of notes ripple from under her hands. Trelane swept Teresa into his arms and burst into a wildly gyrating waltz with her.

"Captain, how far do we go along with this charade?"

It was Sulu's question. Kirk's response was tightly grim. "Until we can think our way out of here. Meanwhile, we'll accept his hospitality . . ."

McCoy snorted with disgust. "Hospitality!" He replaced his laden plate on the table. "You should try his food, Jim. Straw would be tastier than this pheasant. As to the brandy in this glass, plain water has more taste. Nothing he has served has any taste at all."

Spock spoke meditatively. "Food that has no flavor. Wine that has no taste. Fire that gives no heat. Added up, it would seem to suggest that, though Trelane knows all the Earth forms, he knows nothing whatever of their substance."

"And if he's that fallible, he can't be all-powerful. That means he's got something helping him."

"I agree, sir," Spock said.

"A machine. A device—something which does these things for him." Kirk's eyes narrowed as he watched the cavorting Trelane halt his dance briefly in order to adore himself in the walled mirror. "Ah, my dear," he cried to

60

Teresa, "don't we make a graceful pair . . . except for one small detail. That dress you wear hardly matches this charming scene!" Then, Trelane, his eyes fixed on the mirror, lifted that hand of his. Teresa vanished—and immediately reappeared. She was wearing the billowing silks of a luxurious eighteenth-century gown. Diamond bracelets sparkled on her gloved arm; and in her hair glittered a pointed tiara of brilliants.

"Now that's more what we want!" Trelane shouted in delight. "I, the dashing warrior—and you, his elegant lady!"

It was another too impressive demonstration of his extraordinary powers. McCoy's voice was tight. "Three thousand years ago, he would have been considered a god . . . a little god of war." He gave a short, angry laugh. "How suprised the ancients would have been to see—not the grim-visaged brute they visualized as a war god—but a strutting dandy, spreading his peacock's tail in a mirror!"

Kirk echoed the word. "Mirror. That mirror is part of his audience. It's a piece of his ego. He never wanders far from it."

"Is it ego?" Spock said. "Or something else?"

"Explain," Kirk said.

"The mirror," Spock said.

"What about it?"

"As you said, sir, he never gets much distance away from it. I suppose it could be just vanity."

"No, Mr. Spock. He's vain enough—but vanity can't account for his dependence on the mirror." He paused. "What kind of machine could do these things?"

Spock said, "An extremely sophisticated one. In addition to the power to create matter from energy, to guide its shape and motion by thought waves, it would have to have a vast memory bank."

Kirk nodded. "Like a computer. Would you say a machine small enough to be contained in this room could be responsible for maintaining this atmosphere, this house?"

"No, Captain. I think not. Such a device would by necessity be immense—immensely powerful to successfully resist the planet's natural atmosphere."

"Good," Kirk said. "I agree. And that leaves me free . . ."

"Free for what, Captain?"

"To do something which will seem very strange to you, Mr. Spock. Don't think that the strain has got me down. I know exactly what I'm doing."

"Which is—?"

For the first time since meeting the Squire of Gothos, Kirk grinned. "I am going to turn his lights off at their source, Mr. Spock." Then he fell silent. As Trelane waltzed by them with Teresa, he spoke again with unusual loudness. "Nobody is to be too upset by what you see. I am addressing my own people. The actions of this being are those of an immature, unbalanced mind!"

Abruptly, Trelane stopped prancing. "I overheard that last remark. I'm afraid I'll have to dispense with you, Captain." As the arm began to lift, Kirk said, "You only heard part of it. I was just getting started, Trelane!"

The creature's eyes brightened with curiosity. "Oh?"

"Yes," Kirk said. "I want you to leave my crewmen alone! *And my crewwomen, too!*" He reached for Teresa, pulled her away from Trelane, and lifting her, set her down behind him. Then he wheeled to face her. "You're not to dance with him any more! I don't like it!"

First, he snatched the diamond tiara from her hair. Then he reached for the bracelets, peeling them off her arm along with her white glove. Flushing, the girl cried, "Captain, please don't think . . ."

Trelane gave a chortle of pleasure. "Why, I believe the good captain is jealous of me!"

"Believe what you like," Kirk said. "Just keep your hands off her!"

Trelane was staring at him. "How curiously human," he said. "How wonderfully barbaric!"

Taut, no longer acting, Kirk said, "I've had enough of your attentions to her!"

"Of course you have. After all, it's the root of the matter, isn't it, Captain? We males fight for the attention, the admiration, the possession of women—"

Kirk struck him across the face with Teresa's glove. "If fighting is what you want, you'll have it!"

Trelane gave a leap of joy. "You mean—you are challenging me to a duel?" Eyes dancing, he cried, "This is even better than I'd planned. I shall not shirk an affair of

62

honor!" Skipping like a lamb in spring, he ran over to the gleaming box that hung among the weapons displayed over the fireplace. He removed it, lifting its lid. "A matched set," he said. "A matched set exactly like the one that slew your heroic Alexander Hamilton."

Bowing, he presented the box to Kirk. On its velvet lining reposed two curve-handled, flintlock dueling pistols.

Trelane took one. He pointed it at Kirk's head. "Captain," he said, "it may momentarily interest you to know that I never miss my target."

He moved over to take up his position at one side of the room. As he checked the mechanism of his pistol, McCoy, Sulu and the others gathered in an anxious group behind Kirk. He waved them back, thinking, "I know what I'll have to report to the log. Weaponless, powerless, our only hope of escape with the *Enterprise* is playing his games with this retardate of Gothos." He looked up from the absurdity of the ancient dueling pistol. His adversary had a look of rapturous enchantment on his face.

"Fascinating!" he cried ecstatically. "I stand on a Field of Honor. I am party to an actual human duel!"

"Are you ready, Trelane?"

"Quite ready, Captain. We shall test each other's courage—and then—" the voice thickened— "we shall see. . ."

Kirk started to lift his pistol when Trelane cried, "Wait! As the one challenged, I claim the right of the first shot."

"We shoot *together*," Kirk said.

Trelane was querulous. "It's *my* game—and *my* rules." Raising his gun, he aimed it straight at Spock. "But if you need to be persuaded . . ."

When you were dealing with a moral idiot, it was morally idiotic to take heroic stands. "All right," Kirk said. "You shoot first."

"Captain—" Spock was protesting. But Kirk had already lowered his pistol. And Trelane, craving the heroic limelight momentarily focused on Kirk, raised his gun above his head and fired a shot harmlessly into the ceiling.

He was so enraptured by the glory of the figure he cut in his own imagination that he couldn't contain his pleasure. "And now, Captain—how do you say it?—my fate is in your hands." He shut his eyes with a beatific smile; and tearing open his shirt front, exposed his chest to whatever shot, whatever Fate had in store for him.

What Fate had in store for him was surprise. Instead of sending a bullet into Trelane's chest, Kirk sent one, smack! into the center of the mirror on the wall. The glass shattered. And explosively, from behind it, burst a tangle of electronic circuitry, mingled with broken grids and wire-disgorging cables. Something flashed, hissing viciously, spitting blue sparks.

Trelane screamed. He ran to the spark-showering mirror, screaming, "What have you done? What have you done?"

"The machine of power," Spock said very quietly.

It burned out quickly. Above their heads, the rows of candles in the chandelier flickered and died. A grayish, bleak twilight crept into the room. In the grate, the heatless fire was extinct, its passing marked only by a puff of evil-smelling smoke.

Trelane shrieked at the sight of the suddenly dead room. "You've ruined everything!" He sank down on the harpsichord bench; and his elbows, leaned back against its keyboard, evoked a hideously discordant jangle, shrill, ear-splitting.

Beside Kirk, struggling with his communicator, De Salle said, "Captain, subspace interference is clearing . . ."

"Contact the ship!"

Trelane had partially recovered himself. Still torn between contempt for Kirk and admiration, the Squire of Gothos indulged himself in an objective comment. "The remarkable treachery of the human species," he said—and getting up, walked over to the wall bedecked with the blackened ruins of the mirror. Watching him, Kirk said, "Go on, Trelane! Look at it! It's over! Your power is blanked out! You're finished!"

For the first time, genuine feeling triumphed over the emotional theatricality of the Squire of Gothos. He looked somberly at Kirk. "You have earned my wrath," he said. "Go back to your ship! Go back to it! Then prepare. All of you, you are dead men . . . you in particular, Captain Kirk!"

He had begun to move toward the burnt space which

had held the wall mirror. As he reached it, he was gone. Kirk, just a step behind him, was brought up against a blank wall. He stepped back from it, turning to his people. "Everyone! We're getting out of here—and *now!*"

His voice was hoarse as he spoke into his communicator. "This is the captain, *Enterprise!* Commence beaming us up! Make it maximum speed!"

Scott gave their beam-up maximum speed. Kirk left the Transporter Room for the bridge with the same variety of leg haste. In his chair, he quickly reached for the intercom. "Scotty, full power acceleration from orbit!"

"Full power, sir."

The ship leaped forward, and on the viewing screen the crescent-shaped bulk that was Gothos began to dwindle in size.

Kirk said, "Set sourse for Colony Beta Six, Mr. Sulu."

"Laid in, sir."

"Warp Factor One at the earliest possible moment." Sulu said, "Standing by to warp, sir."

Uhura, back with her panels, turned. "Shall I send a full report to Space Fleet Command, Captain?"

Kirk frowned. "Not yet. Not until we're well out of his range. Our beam might be traced."

Spock spoke from his computer post. "Can we know what his range is, sir?"

"We can make an educated guess. At this point—" Kirk had strode over to Spock's assortment of star maps and was directing a forefinger at a spot on one of them. "This is where we first detected the solar system." He was about to return to his chair when he noted Teresa, still wearing the panniered gown of flowered silk. His look of admiration roused her to the realization of its incongruity.

"Sir," she said, "may I take a moment to change, now that the ball is over?"

Kirk smiled at her. "You may—but you'll have to give up that highly becoming garment for scientific analysis, Yeoman Ross."

She flushed. And he tore his eyes away from the vision she made to look back at the viewing screen. Gothos had grown smaller and smaller. Even as he watched, it was lost to sight.

Uhura, the relaxation of her relief in her voice, said, "Still no sign of pursuit, sir. Instruments clear."

Sulu, turning his head, said, "Captain, we are about to warp"—and at the same moment De Salle gave a shout.

"Screen, sir! Large body ahead!"

Just a moment ago the screen had been empty. Kirk stared at its new inhabitant; and De Salle, jumping to his feet, yelled, "Collision course, sir!"

Tight-lipped, Kirk said, "Helm hard to port!"

The bridge crew staggered under the push by the sharp turn. All eyes were fixed on the screen where the crescent-shaped image loomed larger and larger. Then the *Enterprise* had veered away from it. A mutter came from the stunned De Salle. "That was the planet Gothos," he said.

Kirk whirled to Sulu. "Mr. Sulu, have we been going in a circle?"

"No, sir! All instruments show on course . . ."

De Salle gave another yell. "It's Gothos again, Captain!"

The planet had once more appeared on the screen. Kirk barked the evasive order—and again people staggered under the centrifugal force of the ship's abrupt turn. The image of the planet, shrunken on the screen, suddenly enlarged once again. Without order, Sulu put the ship into a vertiginous turn-maneuver. As they came out of it, Spock said, "Cat and mouse game."

"With Trelane the cat," Kirk said tightly.

De Salle, his capacity for intense reaction exhausted, said, low-voiced, "There it is, sir—dead ahead . . ."

On the screen the planet showed red, wreathed by fiery mists. It seemed to boil, noxious, hideously ulcerous with its eruptive skin. Kirk, his jaw set, spoke, "Ninety degrees starboard, Mr. Sulu!"

But though Sulu moved his helm controls, the planet held its place on the screen, always increasing its size.

"We're turning, Captain," Sulu cried. "We're turning —but we're not veering away from it!"

Kirk shouted. "Ninety subport, Mr. Sulu. Adjust!"

What was happening on the screen continued to happen on it. Desperate, Sulu cried, "A complete turn, sir— and we're still accelerating toward the planet!"

Dry as dust, Spock said, "Or it toward us."

Kirk was staring in silence at the screen. "That's *it!*" he said. He wheeled his chair around. "We will decelerate into orbit! We will return to orbit! Prepare the Transporter Room!"

McCoy spoke for the first time. "You're not going down there, Captain! You can't do it, Jim!"

Kirk got up. "I *am* going down, Doctor McCoy. And I *am* going to delight my eyes again with the sight of our whimsical General Trelane. And if it takes wringing his neck to make him let my ship go . . ." He was at the bridge elevator. "Mr. Spock, stand by communicators. If you receive no message from me in one hour, leave this vicinity. At once. Without any sentimental turning back for me."

There was comfort in Spock's quiet nod. No heroics, no weakening sympathy. Just the perception of a reality, a necessity clear to each of them. Spock, his friend.

On a wall in Trelane's drawing room was the shadow of a gallows, dark, implicating. Kirk ignored it. For otherwise, the room was unchanged. Logs burned in the fireplace. The light of candles was refracted from the crystals of its chandelier. The mirror on the wall had been restored, its glass now protected by a heavy wire-mesh shield.

A heavily portentous voice said, "The prisoner may approach the bench."

It was Trelane. He had doffed his military glories for the graver garb of Law's upholders. He wore the white periwig of England's servants of jurisprudence, the black silk robes of a high court judge. He was writing something with a goose-quill pen on some parchment-looking document. The gallows noose—shadow or substance?—seemed to droop over Kirk.

"Trelane . . . !" Kirk said.

Nobody can be so solemn as an idiot. And Trelane, an essential idiot, was very solemn. Solemn and dangerous. In a voice that dripped with unction, he said, "Any attempt at demonstrations will weigh against you with the court. And this time my instrumentality is unbreakable, Captain Kirk."

"My neck seems to be threatened by your court, Trelane. And your neck—is it so very safe?"

A flicker of irritation passed over the heavy-jowled face.

"The absurdity of inferior beings!" said Trelane. He picked up the parchment. "And now, Captain James Kirk, you stand accused of the high crimes of treason, of conspiracy, of attempt to foment insurrection." His periwig must have itched him for he pushed it up, giving himself the look of a slighly drunken, white-haired Silenus. "How do you plead?" he said.

"I haven't come here to plead in your 'court,' Trelane."

The Squire of Gothos sat back, tapping his quill pen against his table. "I must warn you that anything you say has already been taken down in evidence against you."

It was like *Alice in Wonderland*. It was like Looking-Glass Land, where what seems to be is not and what is not appears to be the fact. Reaching for sanity, Kirk said, "I came here for one purpose. I want my ship returned to me."

Irrelevant," Trelane said, giving his periwig an irritated push.

"We made you angry by our will to survive. Is that it?" Kirk said.

Trelane drew a tremulous finger across his upper lip. "Irrelevant," he said. "A comment entirely uncalled for."

"Sure, *that's it*," Kirk retorted. "Then vent your anger on me alone! *I* was the one who led the others—and I was the one who shot out your mirror machine . . ."

For the first time, rage seemed to overwhelm vanity in Trelane. His voice thickened. "And did you really think I wouldn't have more mediums of instrumentality at my command?"

"I took that chance. And I'll accept the price of chancing wrong—"

Trelane rose. "Then you do admit the charges. This court has no choice in fixing punishment. You will hang by the neck until you are dead, dead, dead. Have you any last request?"

Kirk gave a great shout of laughter. "If you think I'm going to stick my head in that noose . . ."

Trelane's hand moved—and Kirk found himself standing under the gallows, its noose, real, heavy, rough around his throat. Trelane, reaching for a black executioner's mask, regarded him plaintively. "This really is becoming tiresome. It's much too easy."

Kirk freed himself from the noose. "Easy!" he yelled. "That's your whole problem, Trelane! Everything comes too easy to you! You don't ever have to *think!* So you lose opportunities. You're enjoying your sense of power right now—but the chance to experience something really unique? You're wasting it! Where's the sport in a simple hanging? In making a rope do your killing for you?"

"Sport?" Trelane echoed. Suddenly his face cleared. He clapped his hands. "Oh, I am intrigued! Go on, Captain! What do you suggest?"

"A personal conflict between us . . . with the stakes a human life—*mine!*"

"What an inspired idea! We need something more fanciful—a truly royal hunt, maybe." He gestured toward the windows. "You go out and hide from me. In the forest . . . anywhere you like . . . and I will seek you out with—*this!*" He wrenched a sword from the scabbard in front of him, brandishing it ferociously. "How does that strike you, Captain? Truly sporting?"

"Yes," Kirk said. "But you must make the game worth my while. While we play it, free my ship."

Trelane sniffed. "Always back to your ship. Oh, very well. If it will lend spice to the pursuit . . ."

Kirk broke into a run, making a dash for a window. He brought up in a copse of vividly green bushes. With desperate haste, he flipped open his communicator. *"Enterprise! Enterprise,* can you hear me? Get the ship away fast! Fast as you can! I'll try to gain you the time you need—"

He stopped. Trelane had burst through the copse, slashing at leaves with his sword. "Ah, ha!" he screamed, "I see you!" But Kirk, diving, had rolled down the slant of a small knoll. Trelane's sword flashed over his head—and in his frantic scramble for the shelter of a heavy-trunked tree, he dropped his communicator.

"You must try harder, Captain!" The sword-point pricked Kirk's arm. He rose from his crouch behind the tree to tear a branch away from it. It struck straight and true on Trelane's sword arm. The weapon flew out of his hand; and Kirk, grabbing it up, slashed at Trelane with all his two-handed strength.

It cut right through him, leaving no sign of wound or of blood. Horrified, Kirk stared—but Trelane, still playing the role of gallant sportsman, merely said, *"Touché,* Captain. I confess you've scored first. But after all, I've never played this game before . . ."

He vanished. Kirk, still shaking, ducked behind a screen of brush. Under it, he saw the gleaming metal of his dropped communicator. *"Enterprise . . . !"*

"En garde!"

Trelane had reappeared, sword lifted. Barely in time, Kirk broke for cover behind a hedge. Then, stooping, he burst out of its shelter to make for the door between the two stone griffins.

"Tallyho!"

The fatuous Squire of Gothos had spotted him. Kirk wheeled to his right—and a stone wall erected itself before him. He whirled to his left; and another blocked his way. Trapped, he backed up against the door of Trelane Hall; and its proprietor, triumph giving his face a look of gorged repletion, said, "Ah, Captain, you made a noble fight of it!" A dribble of saliva issued from the thick lips. "But you are beaten. Down, Captain. Down to me on your knees."

Kirk spoke, the sword against his throat. "You have won nothing.".

"I have! I could run you through! I order you to your knees. I order it!" Trelane lunged with his sword; but Kirk, seizing it, tore it out of his hand; and in one snap over his knee, broke it. He tossed the pieces aside.

"You broke it!" Trelane wailed. "You broke my sword! But I won't have it. I'll blast you out of existence with a wave of my hand!"

Kirk struck him sharply across the face; and Trelane, shrieking, "I'll fix you for that!" squeezed the trigger of the phaser that had suddenly appeared in his hand. A murderously disintegrating ray darted from its muzzle—and at the same moment a woman's voice called "Trelane!"

"No! No!" Trelane howled, running down the steps of his Hall's entrance. Two globes of light hung in the air at their foot. "No! Go away!" he yelled. "You said I could have this planet for my own!" The spheres of light, one slightly smaller than the other, sparkled with an irides-cence of rainbow colors.

Trelane was shouting at them. "You always stop me just when I'm having fun!"

"If you cannot take proper care of your pets, you can-not have any pets," said the female voice.

Trelane burst into tears. "But you saw! I was win-ning! I would have won. I would, I would, I would." But even as he wept, he was dwindling, a shape losing sub-stance, collapsing in on itself. Then he was only an empti-ness in the air.

Kirk looked skyward as though seeking an explana-tion of the inexplicable. "Where are you?" he cried. "Who is Trelane and who are you?"

"You must forgive our child," said the woman's voice. "The fault is ours for overindulging him. He will be pun-ished."

A stern male voice spoke. "We would not have let him intercept you had we realized your vulnerability. For-give us, Captain. We will maintain your life-support condi-tions while you return to your ship. Please accept our apol-ogies."

Kirk flung out his hands toward the two spheres. "Can't you tell me . . . ?" Then, like Trelane, they were gone. After a long moment, he broke out his communica-tor. "Captain to *Enterprise*. Captain calling the *Enter-prise* . . ."

He shut his eyes at the sound—the familiar sound of Spock's voice. "Captain, we are receiving you—"

Kirk gave a last look around him at Trelane's domain —its greenery, the two stone griffins, the appalling solitude of its loneliness in the midst of the Gothos hell. "Beam me up," he said. "Mr. Spock, we're free to leave here."

It was a singularly thoughtful Kirk who gave the order for normal approach procedures to Colony Beta 6. He was glad when Spock left his station to come to the command chair. Somehow he'd known that Spock alone could recon-cile him to the paradoxes of his recent encounter with the Squire of Gothos.

"I am entering," Spock said, "our recent . . . uh . . . interesting experience into the library computer banks, Captain. But I am puzzled."

"Puzzled—you, Mr. Spock?" For a moment the old quizzicalness played across Kirk's face. "I am surprised. I am amazed that you admit it. Explanation, please . . ."

Spock said, "General, or Squire Trelane, Captain. How do we describe him? Pure mentality? A force of intellect? Embodied energy? Superbeing? He must be classified, sir."

Kirk stared unseeingly at his board. "Of course, Mr. Spock. Certainly, he must be classified. Everything must be classified—or where would we be?"

"But I am somewhat at a loss . . ." Spock said.

"A god of war, Mr. Spock?"

"I hardly think . . ."

"Or . . . a small boy, Mr. Spock. And a very naughty one at that."

"It will make a strange entry in the library banks, sir."

"He was a very strange small boy. But on the other hand, he probably was doing things comparable, in their way, to the same mischievous pranks you played when you were a boy."

"Mischievous pranks, Captain?"

"Dipping little girls' curls in inkwells . . . stealing apples . . . tying cans on a dog's—" He broke off, sensing Spock's growing dismay. Where, in the universe, was another Spock to be found—the one you could trust to the end for reasons that had no relation to the ordinary human ones? Kirk grinned. "Excuse me, Mr. Spock. I should have known better. You were never a mischievous small boy."

"As you say, Captain," Spock said.

Back at his station, he cocked a puzzled eyebrow at Kirk. Kirk smiled at him. Spock, lifting the other eyebrow, returned to his computer. And the *Enterprise,* course set, oblivious of the manifold temptations of deep space, sped on to its assignation with Colony Beta 6.

Wink of an Eye

(Arthur Heinemann and Lee Cronin)

In the space fronting the handsome building of unidentified metal, a fountain flung its sparkle of spray into the air. Kirk, abstracted, watched Security Guard Compton taking samples of its water. Nearby, McCoy was scanning the plaza's periphery with his tricorder. Necessary but time-consuming occupations, Kirk thought. And useless. They had done nothing to locate the source of that distress call that had forced their beam-down to this unexplored planet calling itself Scalos.

With abrupt impatience, he opened his communicator. "Kirk to *Enterprise*. Lieutenant Uhura, does the location of that distress signal exactly correspond to this area?"

"Yes, sir. And I am receiving visual contact with the Scalosians. I can't see you on the viewing screen but I can see them."

"Check coordinates, Lieutenant."

"The coordinates correspond, sir."

His impatience grew. "There are no Scalosians, Lieutenant. Apart from our landing party, there is nobody here."

"Their distress call is very strong, sir. They are begging for immediate assistance."

"Check circuits for malfunction. Captain out."

He looked up to meet McCoy's nod. "There *must* be a malfunction, Jim. This is a barren world—hardly any vegetation; no apparent animal life."

As though to contradict him, a shrill mosquito whine sounded near Kirk's head. He struck the invisible insect away. "But there's some kind of insect life," he said.

"My tricorder doesn't register it."

"My ears did," Kirk retorted. He dropped the subject for Spock, rounding a corner of the strangely-fluted metal building, was approaching them. "Anything, Mr. Spock?"

"Evidently a civilization of high order, Captain, rating number seven on the Industrial Scale. Humanoid in appearance, according to paintings. An abundance of literature which I shall have translated and processed. Certain structures hold signs of recent occupancy. Other ones apparently long abandoned."

"But no sign of present life," Kirk said.

As he spoke, he noted that Compton, rinsing his hands in the fountain's jet, had lifted one to knock away some unseen annoyance at his ear. At the same moment, he again heard the mosquito whine. He had to make an effort to concentrate on what Spock was saying. ". . . indication of life forms of a highly unusual intermittent nature. They have neither discernible shape nor location. A most puzzling phenomenon, sir."

"The Scalosians *were* here," Kirk said. "We saw them on the viewing screen, Mr. Spock. Lieutenant Uhura can still see them. She's still getting their distress call. What happened to them?"

"At this moment I cannot answer that, Captain."

"Mr. Spock, I want you to make a complete survey of this planet. You will use all the ship's instruments—"

He broke off at McCoy's shout. "Jim! Compton's gone! Look over there! Compton's gone!"

Emptiness was where the guard had been stooping at the fountain. McCoy was staring at its feathered plume of water dazedly. "Compton—gone," he said again.

"Bones!" Kirk said. "Snap out of it! What happened?"

McCoy's shocked eyes veered to his. "He . . . was stowing vials of that fountain's water in his shoulder bags

74

. . . when he vanished. I was looking straight at him—and then he wasn't there. He wasn't there, Jim. He . . . just wasn't there . . ."

Had the Scalos distress signal been real? Maybe unreal like its inhabitants. Kirk, entering the *Enterprise* bridge, barked an inconsequential order to an unremembered crew member. As he sat down in his command chair, he said, "Lieutenant Uhura, start a replay of that distress call." Then he hit a switch. "Mr. Scott, are all Transporter controls still in functioning order?"

"Aye, sir. Is Mr. Spock still down on the planet's surface?"

"He's in Sickbay. Dr. McCoy is running a check on the landing party." His attention, used to dispersing itself to note any significant movement in the bridge, had registered Uhura's look as she struggled with her dials. "What is it, Lieutenant?"

She was frowning. "Malfunction, sir." She touched a switch—and her frown deepened. "Now it's corrected itself."

Sulu spoke. "Captain, there's some trouble on the hangar deck. Controls are frozen."

"Have repair crews been assigned?"

"Yes, sir."

Kirk shot a look of inquiry at Uhura. She nodded. "The tape of the distress call is ready, sir."

Spock had quietly returned to his station. Now he turned to look at the viewing screen. An upside-down image took shape on it. Then, righting itself, it showed a proud, strong male face. Its lips moved. "Those of us who are left have taken shelter in this area. We have no explanation for what has been happening to us. Our number is now five . . ."

The face on the screen took on human height and breadth. The figure moved; and around it appeared the four other Scalosians, two of them women. One was surpassingly lovely. The whole impression created by the group was that of a cultured, singularly handsome people, peaceful in purpose. Their spokesman went on. "I am Rael. We were once a nation of nine hundred thousand, this city alone holding—"

"Freeze it," Kirk said.

Uhura immobilized the tape and Spock, swinging around, said, "Perhaps this distress call was prerecorded —and what we received was a taped signal."

"Mr. Spock, the fact remains that when we beamed down, we could not find these people. They *were* there— now they're *not* there. Nor is crewman Compton."

"Some force or agent only partially discernible to our instruments may have been responsible, Captain."

Kirk nodded. "Mr. Sulu, I want this ship on standby alert while we continue the investigation." But Sulu had turned an anxious face to him. "I have a reading, sir, that our deflectors are inoperative. They do not respond to controls."

"Scotty, assist," Kirk said. He got up to go over to Spock's chair. "Mr. Spock, ever since we beamed back up from Scalos, we have suffered a series of malfunctions. I wish an investigation and an explanation. I want—"

McCoy's voice interrupted. "McCoy to Captain Kirk. The Captain's presence for examination is requested."

"Can't it wait, Bones?"

"Your orders, Jim. You're the last one."

"What do you read so far?"

"Can we discuss it in Sickbay?"

Moving to the elevator, Kirk said, "Mr. Spock, you have the con." But the elevator doors, instead of whooshing open at his approach, remained shut. Kirk wheeled, shouting, "Is this another malfunction?"

Spock jabbed hastily at buttons: and after a long moment, the doors opened slowly, grudgingly. Kirk was still fuming as he jerked off his shirt in Sickbay. "Bones! What did your examinations of the others turn up?"

"All normal. Whatever caused Compton's disappearance didn't affect anyone else."

"Has anyone experienced anything unusual since beaming back up?"

"No mention of it. No, Jim."

But Nurse Chapel looked up from the sheet she was draping over Kirk's midriff. "Yet something's going on, Captain. All the medical supply cabinets have been opened."

76

Kirk sat up. "Anything missing?"

"Just disordered. As if everything had been picked up and examined."

Once again that insect whine sounded close to Kirk's ear. He waited a moment before he said, "Bones, could something be causing me to hallucinate?" The urgency in his voice startled McCoy out of his concentration on his medical panels. He turned. "How—hallucinate? What do you mean?"

"Twice," Kirk said, "I've felt something touch me. Nothing was there. I just felt it again. Did I just fancy it?"

"There's nothing physically wrong with you, Jim."

"I asked you a question. Am I hallucinating?"

McCoy left his panels. "No."

Kirk leaped from the medical table. "Then we *did* beam something aboard! Something has invaded this ship!" He was making for the intercom when the alarm of a red alert sounded. Over the shrieking of its sirens, he cried, "Captain to bridge! Mr. Spock, come in!"

Spock didn't come in. Minutes passed before Kirk could hear the voice, faint, blurred. "Captain, I have a reading from the life support center . . ."

"Spock, I can't hear you! Check circuits. Is it a malfunction?"

More minutes passed. Then it was Uhura speaking, her voice also dimmed and distorted. " . . . intercom system breaking down rapidly . . ."

Kirk felt the sweat breaking out on his forehead. "Lieutenant, issue a shipwide order! Use communicators instead of the intercom. Arm all crewmen with phaser pistols. Spock, come in!"

The words were a jumble. "Reading . . . life support . . . center. Alien . . . substances . . . introduced . . ."

Kirk was shouldering into his shirt. "Mr. Spock, meet me in the life support center! On the double! Captain to Security! Armed squad to life support center at once!" He was at Sickbay's door when he saw McCoy sway. Christine Chapel, clutching the back of a chair, called, "The oxygen content is dropping, Doctor . . ."

As for Kirk himself, Sickbay, its door, its cabinets, its equipment, were all swimming into blur. He fought the dizziness that threatened to become darkness, struggling to open his communicator. "Bridge! Bridge! Scotty, where are you? Emergency life support!"

Scott's steady voice said. "Emergency on, sir."

Behind him, McCoy and Christine were gulping in lungfuls of healthy air. Kirk's vertigo subsided—and Scott said, "Condition corrected, Captain."

But the cold hand of imminent death had touched Kirk. It was a man of a different discipline who met Spock at the entrance to the life support center. As wordlessly as it was given, he took the phaser, flinging open the door to the center. Its security guards, sprawled on the floor, were kneeing back up to their feet. One, phaser out, charged to his left, only to be flung back and down again by something invisible. Kirk, staring around him, said, "How do you explain that, Mr. Spock?"

The sharp Vulcan eyes scanned their tricorder. "A force field, sir, with the nature of which I am unfamiliar. But I get a reading of alien presences similar to those obtained on the planet. They seem to have no exact location."

"'Life forms of a highly unusual, intermittent nature'." Kirk recalled grimly. "Phasers on stun, everybody. Sweep the area."

Once more came the thin whine. Phaser beams were lacing the corridor outside. Inside, Kirk and Spock edged cautiously forward to the location of the force field. Instead of flinging them back, it yielded to them; but when a guard moved to follow them, he was struck down.

"It would seem they will allow only the two of us in to the life support unit," Spock said. "Take care, Captain."

Kirk took the advice. He opened the heavy door to the unit, his weapon at the ready. At first glance the unit appeared to be its usual self, its complex coils, squat dynamos, its serpentine tubings and compressors arranged in their customary pattern. Then Kirk saw the gleaming metal of the device affixed to one of the dynamos. The metal was fluted like that of the Scalosian building. Though alien in shape and material, the small device had been able to affect the functioning of the huge life support unit.

"Mr. Spock, what is it?"

"I cannot determine, Captain. Perhaps a Scalosian refrigerating system." He scanned the thing with his tricorder.

"It would seem that installation of the device is incomplete, sir. Life support is still operational."

"Disconnect it," Kirk said.

But the hand Spock extended toward the fixture was flung back. Kirk, whipping out his phaser, heard yet again that now familiar whine. "Destroy it, Spock!" he shouted.

As their two phasers fired at the device, their weapons disappeared. One moment, they were hard, tangible in their hands; but the next, they were gone. Both men pushed forward and were thrust strongly back.

"And that wasn't a force field!" Kirk cried. "Something pushed me back. They are in here with us!" He swung around, shouting at the empty air. "You! What are you doing to my ship? Show yourselves!"

The mosquito whine shrilled. They tried again, not lunging this time to the device but approaching it. A hard shove sent them stumbling back.

Spock's voice was dry. "It seems that we may look at their mechanism—but that is all, Captain."

Kirk nodded. "A show of strength." He shouted again to the invisible enemies. "But we'll find a way to dismantle this aggressive engine of yours!"

It was more than a mere show of strength. Back on the bridge, they discovered that key systems over the entire ship had either been crossed or fused. Spock's computer alone was still operational. All doors, including those of the elevators, were jammed open. Scott greeted them with a gloom thick as a Tyneside fog. "Warp engines are losing potency, Captain. We shall be on emergency power soon —a situation that gives us at most one week of survival."

Kirk wheeled to Spock. "Have your readings been fed into the computer bank?"

"Affirmative, Captain."

"Readout."

Flipping a switch, Spock addressed the computer. "Analyze and reply. Have we been invaded?"

"Affirmative."

"Nature and description of enemy forces."

"Data insufficient."

"Purpose of the invasion."

"Immediate purpose, seizure and control of the Fed-

79

eration Starship *Enterprise*. Data insufficient for determination of end purpose."

"Is there a link between this seizure and Compton's disappearance?"

"Data insufficient."

"Are we at present capable of resisting?"

"Negative."

"Recommendations?"

"If incapable of resistance, negotiate for terms."

Listening, Kirk glared at the computer. Then he flushed at his own childishness. The computer was just doing its computer job. But men were not computers. "We will not negotiate for terms," he said. "Scotty, do you concur?"

"Aye, sir."

Spock, giving him an approving nod, said, "What are *your* recommendations, Captain?"

"Coffee," Kirk said. He turned to the pretty yeoman on duty. "Is a round of coffee available to bridge personnel—or have those circuits also been damaged?"

She smiled, adoration in her eyes. It shouldn't have cheered him up—but it did. Challenge hardened his jaw as he looked around him at an air made malevolent by invisible hostility. "Let them take the next step," he said. "The next move is theirs."

His cup of coffee was set on the arm of his chair. He let it wait to cool. Then, as he leaned back in the chair, his hair was suddenly stirred. He stared around him, baffled —and felt soft lips on his. He *was* hallucinating. McCoy was wrong. He put out a tentative hand, exploring the space before him. Shaking his head, he seized his cup and, after drinking its coffee, replaced it on the chair arm. At the same instant, he became abruptly aware of a change of tempo in the voices around him. They sounded too slow, like those from a phonograph that was running down. And the movements of the bridge people—they, too, seemed strangely slowed, lethargic.

He went to Spock. But Spock, who had bent to his computer, seemed unable to reach its hood.

"Mr. Spock, what's wrong?"

The Vulcan didn't answer. He sat perfectly still in his chair. Kirk wheeled, calling, "Scotty!" No reply. Scott appeared to be frozen in the very act of moving a dial. It was then he heard the feminine giggle—a very feminine giggle. It came from his left. He turned. The Scalosian beauty was standing there, her chestnut hair making a dream of her creamy skin. She wore a short garment of golden gauze that clung to a slim body of subliminally provocative appeal. She was laughing at him; and the gleam of her teeth between her rosy lips gave the lie to all poets' talk of "pearls."

Still laughing, she kissed him. She flung her arms around his neck and kissed him. He tried. He tried to remember who he was; the pressing problems of the *Enterprise*, his command responsibilities. But all he succeeded in doing was to remove the lovely arms from his neck.

"Who are you?" he said.

"Deela, the enemy," she said. "Isn't it delicious?"

He had thought he knew women. But nothing in his experience had prepared him for this dazzling combination of mischief and outrageously open attractiveness. *"You're the enemy?"*

She nodded her enchanting head. "Yes. You beamed me aboard yourself when you came up. A ridiculously long process . . ."

"What have you done to my ship?"

"Nothing."

He swung around to gesture to the motionless bridge people. "You call that nothing?"

"They're all right," she said. "They're just what they have always been. It's you who are different."

He stared around him. "Lieutenant Uhura . . . Mr. Sulu . . . every one of them . . ."

"Captain, they can't hear us. To their ears we sound like insects. That's *your* description, you know. Accurate, if unflattering. Really, nothing's wrong with them."

"Then what have you done to me?"

"Changed you. You are like me now. Your crew can't see you because of the acceleration. We both move now in the wink of an eye. There is a dreary scientific term for it —but all that really matters is that you can see me and talk to me and . . ." The creamy eyelids lowered over eyes the color of wet green leaves. ". . . and we can go on from there."

"Why?" Kirk said.

"Because I like you. Didn't you guess?" She came closer to him. She was ruffling his hair now; and he seemed unable to do a thing about it. The situation was out of hand . . . the presence of his crew . . . this public exhibition of endearments . . . her overwhelming beauty . . . his ship's predicament. He seized the caressing hands. They were warm, soft. It wasn't the answer.

"Is it because you like me that you've sabotaged my ship?"

"It hasn't been sabotaged. We just had to make some changes in it to adjust it to our tempo."

" 'We'?"

"Of course. My chief scientist and his men. I'm their Queen. You're going to be their King. You'll enjoy living on Scalos."

"And what happens to my ship—*my* men?"

"Oh, in a few of their moments they'll realize you've vanished. Then they'll look for you. But they won't find you. You're accelerated far beyond their powers to see. So they'll go on without you . . ."

He became conscious that her hands were still in his. He released them. She smiled at him. "Don't be stubborn. You *can't* go back to them. You must stay with me. Is that so dreadful a prospect?"

He reached for his phaser. "I won't kill you—but the 'stun' effect isn't very pleasant."

"Go ahead," she said. "Fire it at me."

He fired the stun button. She stepped aside and the beam passed harmlessly by her. She laughed at the look on his face. "Don't look so puzzled. My reactions are much too fast for such a crude weapon. Besides, I'm quite good at self-defense." She pulled a small instrument from her golden belt. Pointing it at his phaser, she fired it—and its beam tore the phaser out of his hand. "It can be set for stun and destroy, too," she said. "Like yours. Please accept what's happened. There's nothing you can do to change it."

His ship. Suppose he capitulated—and went with her? Went with her on the condition she made the *Enterprise* operational again and removed the device attached to the life support system? Spock could carry on . . .

His face was somber. She saw it set into grim lines

82

and cried, "Don't fret so! You'll feel better about it in a little while. It always happens this way . . . they're all upset at first. But it wears off and they begin to like it. You will, too. I promise . . ."

He turned on his heel and left her. She touched a medallion on the golden belt. "He's on his way to you, Rael. Be gentle with him," she said.

Kirk came at a run down the corridor to the life support center. He found what he expected. The *Enterprise* guards at its door were stiff, rigid. He skirted them; and was starting toward the door when a third guard in the Starship's uniform emerged from a corner. "Compton!" Kirk shouted.

Compton beamed at him. "Captain Kirk! So you made it here!"

"You've been accelerated, haven't you?" Kirk said. "Yes, sir."

"Are they in there? They've got something hooked in to life support— and we've got to get rid of it. Come on!"

But Compton had barred his way with the Scalosian weapon. "Sorry, sir. Entry is forbidden."

"Who gave that order?"

"The commander, sir. You'll have to step back, please."

"*I* am your commander—and I order you to let me in."

"*I* am very sorry, sir. You are no longer my commander."

"Then who is? Deela? Are you working for her?"

Compton reached an arm back into the corner's shadows and drew out the other Scalosian girl. He spoke very earnestly. "At first I refused, sir—but I've never known anyone like Mira. She brought me aboard and I showed them the ship's operations, its bridge controls and life support. I didn't understand at first but I do now. I—I've never been in love before, sir."

Kirk stepped back. Then, lunging at Compton, he chopped the weapon away from him and raced for the door.

In the center, Rael, two other Scalosians beside him, was working on the small device. He looked up as Kirk plunged in. "Stun," he said to one of his men. The weapon came up; and from behind Kirk, pushing him aside, Compton hurled himself at it. His try at protection was too late. The blast caught Kirk. He collapsed. Raging, Rael felled Compton with a blow. "You were ordered to stop him! Why did you disobey?"

Compton's mouth was bleeding. "You wanted to hurt him," he said.

"He was violent and to be subdued. Why did you disobey?"

"He—he was my Captain . . ."

Compton crumpled. "Go to him, Ekor," Rael said. The man with the weapon knelt beside Compton. Mira, who had drifted into the center, joined him. When he looked up, he said, "There is cell damage." The girl, her pretty face curious, stooped over Compton. "Don't be troubled," Rael told her. "Another will be secured for you." Nodding, she strolled out of the door.

It was Uhura who first noticed the empty command chair. "The captain!" she cried. "He's gone! Mr. Spock, the captain's gone! He was sitting there just a minute ago! He'd just drunk his coffee! There's the cup—on the arm of his chair! But where's the Captain?"

Spock had already left his station. "Mr. Sulu, what did you see?"

Sulu turned a bewildered face. "That's what happened, sir. He was there, putting his cup down—and then he wasn't there!"

There was a moment's silence before Spock said, "Mr. Sulu, did you drink coffee when the yeoman brought it around?"

"Yes, sir."

Spock eyed the bridge personnel. "Did anyone else?" he said.

"I had some," Scott said.

One by one Spock lifted their cups, sniffing at them. Then he sniffed at Kirk's.

"Was it the coffee?" Scott cried. "Are we going to vanish, too, like the captain?"

"The residue in these cups must be analyzed before I can answer that, Mr. Scott."

"And by *that* time—" Scott fell silent.

"I suggest," Spock said," that we remember the Captain's words. Make them take the next step. In the meantime we must determine effective countermoves. The con is yours, Mr. Scott. I shall be in the medical laboratory."

Deela sat on the deck in life support center, the head of the still unconscious Kirk in her lap. Rael, at the device, watched her as she smoothed the hair from his forehead. "I told you," she said, "to be gentle with him."

"He was violent. We had to stun him to avoid cell damage."

She looked over to where Compton lay in a neglected huddle. "Who damaged that one? You? I might have known it. I suppose he was violent, too."

"He turned against us," Rael said.

"And you lost your temper."

"He had to be destroyed. He had not completely accepted change. It is a stubborn species."

Deela's eyes were still on Compton. "I know what happens to them when they're damaged. You will control your temper, Rael. I don't want that to happen to mine. If they're so stubborn a species, perhaps they'll last longer."

"It may be."

"I hope so. They all go so soon. I want to keep this one a long time. He's pretty."

"He is inferior, Deela!"

"We disagree, Rael."

"You cannot allow yourself to feel an attachment to such a thing!"

"I can allow myself to do anything I want!" The flare of anger passed as quickly as it had come. "Oh, Rael, don't be that way," she coaxed. "Am I jealous of what you do?"

"I do my duty."

"So do I. And sometimes I allow myself to enjoy it."

As she spoke, Kirk's dazed eyes opened. Under his head he felt the softness of feminine thighs. He shook it to clear it; and looking up, saw Deela smiling at him. "Hello," she said.

He sat up—and recognized Rael. Leaping to his feet, he turned on Deela. "Is this what you wanted us for? To take over our ship?"

She rose in one graceful movement. "We need your help. And you and your ship are supplying it."

"And what does that device of yours have to do with the supply?"

"Hush," she said. "I'll tell you everything you want to know. And you'll approve of it."

"Approve!" he shouted. "We're your prisoners!"

"Hardly," she said. "You're free to go wherever you want."

Kirk rushed to the life support unit. Instead of interfering, Rael stepped aside. "Go ahead, Captain. Our mechanism is not yet completely linked to your support system but it is in operating order. Study it if you wish. I advise you not to touch it."

Kirk's eyes narrowed. He eyed the small device; and spotting its connecting switch, extended a wary hand to it. He snatched it back, the Scalosians watching him expressionlessly. Then, despite the shock of contact with it, he grabbed it boldly with both hands. They froze on it. Deela ran to him; and, careful not to touch the switch herself, released his hands.

"He told you not to touch it!" She folded his numbed palms between hers, warming them. "The cold will soon pass," she said.

Rael spoke. "Our mechanism has its own self-defense arrangement. You should have heeded me."

Kirk jerked his still icy hands from Deela's. He'd had enough of these aliens; and, feeling a sudden compunction for Compton, sprawled and untended in his heap, he went to him quickly to kneel beside him. But what had been the young and vigorous Compton was now withered by age, mummified as though dried by a thousand years of death. He looked up in horror and Rael said, "In your struggle with Compton, you damaged some of his cells. Those newly accelerated to our tempo's level are sensitive to cell damage. They age very rapidly and die."

Kirk got to his feet. "Is this what you have prepared for us?"

"We all die," Rael said. "Even on Scalos."

Kirk looked around at the bland faces. Where was the way back into his own time . . . the time of Spock . . . of McCoy . . . of Scotty? A sense of unut-

86

terable loneliness overwhelmed him. He walked out of the center.

Behind him Deela cried, "Rael, why did you lie to him? He didn't damage the dead one! You did!"

Rael shrugged. "Perhaps he'll be less violent now."

"There was no reason to make him feel worse than he does!"

"What do you care about his feelings?"

She changed her tactics. "Rael," she said, "he's not one of us. You know he's temporary." But Rael still stooped to his work. She sighed; and touching the medallion on her belt, listened. "He's in the medical laboratory trying to communicate with the Vulcan. He likes that one of the pointed ears. His species seems capable of much affection."

"I have noted that," Rael said stiffly.

"Oh, stop sulking! Accept it. We've had to accept it all our lives! Don't make it worse!"

Rael seized her fiercely in his arms. Her hand was reaching to caress his face when she broke free, laughing and breathless. "Not now," she said. "Go back to work."

He didn't. Instead, he watched her as she followed Kirk out of the center. She found the door of the medical laboratory open. Ignoring the rigid figures of Spock and McCoy, she went to the communicator console where Kirk was dictating. "Kirk to Spock," he was saying. "I have fed all facts ascertainable into the computer banks—" He broke off as he saw Deela.

She studied him—a beautiful woman estimating a man for her own reasons. "Go ahead," she said. "It won't accomplish anything. But it may be historically valuable."

Eyes on her, he continued. "Hyper-acceleration is the key, Mr. Spock. We are in their control because of this acceleration. They are able to speed others up to their level as they did to Compton and me. Those so treated then exist at their accelerated tempo, become eventually docile but when—"

"Damaged," Deela said.

Kirk gave her a mock bow. "When damaged, they age incredibly fast as if the accelerated living—"

"Burns them out," Deela said.

"Destroys them. Compton is destroyed. The device affixed to life support produces an icy cold. It is my belief it will turn the *Enterprise* into a gigantic deep-freeze and for purposes the Scalosians alone know—"

"Quite correct," Deela said.

Kirk was ironic. "My opinion has been verified. Their mechanism has it own protective shield, preventing physical contact. I have no means of destroying it. But its destruction is imperative. I am dictating this in the presence of their Queen who has denied none of it. Why she has permitted me to—"

Leaning forward, the cloud of her hair brushing his shoulder, Deela spoke for the record into the communicator.

"Because by the time you hear this, it will be too late. Our mechanism will be activated."

He turned to look at the two stiffened figures of his friends. The ice would creep through the *Enterprise* to stiffen them forever in a shroud of frost. He swung to Deela. "*Why*? Why are you doing this?"

"You really want to know? In a short time, it won't matter to you a bit. You'll be quite happy about it, as Compton was."

"I want to know."

"Oh dear. Your *are* so stubborn. It should be obvious to one with your reasoning powers that we're doing it because we have to." She pushed the shining cloud of hair back. "A long time ago, we used to be like you. Then our country was almost destroyed by volcanic eruptions. The water was polluted and radiation was released. That changed us. It accelerated us . . ."

He waited. It was possible. The long-term effects of radiation were still unpredictable. "The children died," she said. "Most of the women found they couldn't bear any more. All our men had become sterile. We had to mate outside our own people . . ."

A doomed race. Listening, Kirk seemed to know what he was going to hear. He felt a stab of pity. She gave him a sad little smile. "So, whenever a space ship came by, we sent out calls for help. But accelerating their crews to our level burned them out . . ." She came to him and put her head on his shoulder. "Don't you see? Must I give you every detail? We're going to take you down with us. Maybe one or two others of your crew, too. We have to. We'll be kind to you. I *do* like you, you know."

"And the rest of my crew?" Kirk said.

"It's as you said. They'll be kept frozen in a reduced animation we know how to suspend. It won't do them any harm. We'll save them for our future needs. You won't last forever. You know that." At the look on his face, a cry tore from her. "Captain, we have the right to survive!"

"Not at the cost you impose," he said.

"You'd do exactly the same thing! You came charging down into that life support room just as soon as you knew it was threatened! You'd have killed every one of my people if you could have . . ."

"You had invaded my ship! You were endangering my crew!"

"There's no difference!" she cried.

"There's every difference. You are the aggressors!"

"We didn't ask for our situation. We're simply handling it the only way we know how to—the way our parents did and their parents before them . . ."

"Would you call it a real solution?"

She looked at him, silent. "Have you tried any other answer? Deela, tell your scientist to disconnect his construction—to destroy it! I promise you we'll use every skill we have to help you. We'll even move you to another planet if you want that. We'll call on the most brilliant minds in our Federation for help!"

She shook her head. "We *have* tried other ways. We tried to make the transition to your time level. Those who made the attempt died. We're trapped, Captain, just as you are now. I'm sorry for what it's going to do to you but I can't change it. And you can't change me."

The medallion on her belt beeped. She touched it and Rael's voice said, "Go to the Transporter Room, Deela. Signal me when you're there and beam down."

"With the captain?"

She was frowning, concentrated on the medallion—and Kirk grabbed his chance. He pulled his dictated tape partially out of the computer so that Spock would note it. He heard Rael say, "Yes. I'll activate our mechanism and follow you. I'm setting it to allow enough time for all of us to get off the ship. But don't delay, Deela."

Kirk had raced for the lab door. Behind him, Deela shouted, "The captain's gone!"

"Go after him, Deela!"

But his headstart had given him time to make the Transporter Room. He rushed to its console, ripped out some wire; and had it shut again to conceal the damage as Deela ran in.

"Why did you leave me?" she demanded.

"I panicked," Kirk said.

The green eyes swept over him. "I don't believe that," she said.

"Can we leave before he activates your device?" he said.

She looked at him, her smooth brow puckered suspiciously. Then she touched the medallion. "Rael, we're in the Transporter Room. You can—activate."

"Beam him down at once."

Still doubtful, she gestured Kirk to the platform. At the console, she pushed a switch. It swung, limp—and the smile in the green eyes deepened. "What did you do to the Transporter, Captain?"

"Nothing," he said. "It must be what your people did. Try the switch again."

She obeyed. Then she touched the medallion communicator. "The Transporter isn't working," she said quietly.

"What did he do to it?"

She delayed her answer. The impishness glinted in her eyes. She was enjoying herself. It was fun to pretend she didn't know what she knew. "Nothing," she told Rael. "He didn't have time. I think it's a—what do they call it? A malfunction. You'd better not activate yet." She turned to Kirk, the amusement still in her face. "What would you say it is, Captain?"

He assumed a thoughtful look. "Well, our technicians reported a loss of energy. That may be it."

She spoke solemnly to the medallion. "The captain says his technicians—"

"I heard him. Do you expect me to believe him?"

It was the Queen in her who spoke. "*I* expect you to check into all possible causes." She turned the medallion off to smile the impish smile at Kirk. "If I had a suspicious nature," she said, "I'd say you sabotaged the Transporter, Captain. To buy time."

"Of course," he said.

She laughed with delight. "Aren't we the innocent pair? I despise devious people, don't you?"

Kirk nodded gravely. "I believe in honest relationships, myself." He hesitated. "Deela, you've never seen my quarters. Before we leave, wouldn't you like to?"

Their eyes met. "Are they like you?" she said. "Austere, efficient—but in their own way, handsome?"

"Yes," he said.

In his cabin, the first thing she went to was his mirror. "Oh, I look a perfect fright! All this running about has left me a perfect fright, hasn't it?"

She lifted a brush from the dresser and flung her head over, the shining hair cascading to the floor. She parted the chestnut curtain with a finger, peeking at him. Then she laughed, tossed the hair back and began to brush it, a delicious woman attracting what she knows her preening has attracted. An electric spark flashed between them.

"Are you married, Captain?"

"No."

"No family, no attachments? Oh, I see. You're married to your career and never look at a woman."

"You're mistaken," he said. "I look, if she's pretty enough."

"I wondered when you'd say something nice to me. Am I more presentable now?"

"A bit," he said.

She was facing him, the brush still in her hand. "It was quite delightful kissing you when you couldn't see me. But now that you do see me, don't you think . . . ?"

He strode to her, took her in his arms and kissed her. She drew back—but he had felt her body tremble. Her arms were reaching for his neck when she whirled out of his embrace, her weapon out. "Unfair!" she cried. "To try and take it in the middle of a kiss!"

She thrust it back into her belt. "But I'll forgive you. I'd have been disappointed in you if you *hadn't* tried to take it!"

"Was I too crude?" Kirk said.

"Just don't try it again, that's all. You're so vulnerable to cell damage. All I have to do is scratch you." She held up pink nails. Then she lifted his arms and placed them around her waist. "You'll come around to our way of thinking sooner or later. And it will be better sooner than later. That's a promise."

In the medical lab, Spock, still functioning in normal time, was about to insert a tape of his own into the computer when McCoy called him. "Have a look at this, Spock. There's no question about it. The same substance is in the captain's coffee as in the Scalosian water. But not a trace of it in the other cups."

Spock spoke to Christine. "Nurse, program that information and see if we can isolate counteragents."

A mosquito whined. Spock, striking at air, turned to McCoy. "Did you just hear—"

"I've been hearing that whine ever since we beamed down to Scalos."

"We brought it with us. And I know what it is. I shall be on the bridge." They stared after him, puzzled, as he raced out of the lab. He was still running when he brought up short on the bridge. "Lieutenant Uhura, replay that Scalosian distress call on my viewer!"

"Yes, sir."

Rael's image appeared on the screen. Spock leaned forward in his chair, waiting for the voice. It came. "Those of us who are left have taken shelter in this area. We have no explanation for what has been happening to us. Our number is now five . . ."

It was enough. Spock twisted a dial on the viewer; and the voice, rising in pitch, became incoherent babble, went higher still until it turned into recognizable whine. Spock slowed the voice back into words, lifted it up again into the whine—and nodded. On the screen, the image, rushed faster and faster, had first blurred. Then it vanished.

"So," Spock said to nobody.

Back in the lab, McCoy had made a discovery, too. Banging away the whining mosquito at his ear, he spoke into the intercom. "McCoy to Spock."

"Spock, here."

"Did you leave a tape in the computer? I've tried reading it but I get nothing but that whine . . ."

"Bring it to the bridge at once, Doctor."

Kirk's voice. They listened to it on their separate edges of eternity, each of them reading his own fate in Compton's and Kirk's.

". . . Its destruction is imperative. I am dictating this in the presence of their Queen who has denied none of it. Why she has permitted me—"

Deela's voice came. "Because by the time you hear this, it will be too late. The mechanism will be activated . . ."

Silence fell over the bridge people. Spock leaned swiftly to his console. "I read no change in life support," he said. "Lieutenant Uhura, alert the rest of the crew."

Scott rose and went to him. "We could use phasers to cut through the wall, bypass the force field and get to that mechanism . . ."

"Mr. Scott, we cannot cope with them on our time level."

"Is there a way to cope with them on theirs?"

"A most logical suggestion, Mr. Scott. Please stand by in the Transporter Room. Dr. McCoy, I should appreciate your assistance."

They left with him, their faces blank with bewilderment. Uhura followed them with her eyes. "Mr. Sulu, if nothing has happened yet, wouldn't it mean that the captain has managed to buy time, somehow?"

"Yes," Sulu said. "But how much?"

Rael had restored sufficient energy to the Transporter for a beam-down. But his success had a bitter taste. His fancy persisted in tormenting him with present and future images of Deela with Kirk. Finally, he touched his own medallion.

"Deela . . ."

She didn't answer. Languorously, she was combing her hair to rights before Kirk's mirror. He watched her from a chair. Then he got up, smiling at her reflection in the mirror. As he kissed the back of her neck, she turned full into his arms.

"Deela!"

93

Rael stood in the cabin doorway. The hot fury in him exploded. He reached for her; and seizing a lamp, hurled it at Kirk. Kirk ducked it. Cell damage! In his accelerated state, this could be no ordinary fight. Deela screamed, "Rael, stop it! Don't hurt him! Rael! Captain, get out . . ."

Grabbing her weapon, she fired it at the lamp. But Rael lunged at Kirk again, barehanded. She fired again, spinning him around with the force beam. "That's enough!" she cried. "Did he damage you, Captain?"

"No."

"How very fortunate for you, Rael! Don't try anything like that again!"

"Then don't torment me. You know what I feel."

"I don't care what you feel. Keep that aspect of it to yourself. What I do is necessary, and you have no right to question it." She paused to add more quietly, "Allow me the dignity of liking the man I select."

He stood sullen but subdued. "Is the Transporter repaired?" she said.

"I have more work to do."

"Then do it." He left. She remained silent, more depressed by the scene than she cared to show. After a long moment, she spoke. "He loves me. I adored him when I was a child. I suppose I still do." She made an effort to recover their former mood. "I must say, you behaved better than he did."

"I hope so," Kirk said.

Something in his manner startled her. "What did you say?"

"That I hope I behaved well."

She was staring at him. "And nothing troubles you now?"

"Why are we here?"

"Our leaving was delayed. Don't you remember? You damaged the Transporter."

"That was wrong," Kirk said.

"It certainly was."

"But we are going to Scalos?"

"Do you want to?"

"Yes."

94

"What about your crew? Aren't you worried about them?"

"They'll be all right here."

Her mouth twisted with distaste. "What's the matter?" Kirk said.

"You've completely accepted the situation, haven't you? You even like it."

"Am I behaving incorrectly?"

"No." Then she burst out petulantly. "Oh, I liked you better before! Stubborn, independent . . . and irritating! Like Rael!"

"Those are undesirable qualities," Kirk said.

But she was brooding over her discovery. "Maybe that's why I liked you so much. Because you were like him."

The muscles of Kirk's face ached under the blandness of his smile. But he held it. She touched her medallion. "Rael, you don't have to worry about him. He's made the . . . adjustment."

McCoy was examining the vial of liquid he had processed. "It's finished," he told Spock wearily.

Spock took the vial; and, mixing some of its contents with the Scalosian water, exposed the result to an electronic device. "It counteracts the substance most effectively, Doctor."

"Under laboratory conditions. The question is, will it work in the human body? And the second question is, how do we get it to the captain?"

Spock poured some of the Scalosian water into a glass. He lifted the glass in a toast to McCoy. "By drinking their water." He drained the glass.

"Spock!" You don't know what the effects—"

But Spock was savoring the taste. "It is . . . somewhat stimulating." He paused. "And yes, Doctor, you seem to be moving very slowly. Fascinating."

He winked out. McCoy sank down in a chair, his eyes on the vacancy where Spock had stood.

Rael, his face intent, twisted a knob on his refrigerating mechanism. When it flared into red life, he adjusted another one. He nodded to himself as it began to pulsate, its throb dimming the lights of the life support unit. He touched his communicator medallion. "The arrangement is activated, Deela. Go to the Transporter Room and beam-down at once. The others have already left."

Scott was at the console. Unseeing, unmoving, he didn't turn as Kirk entered the room with Deela. Time, time, Kirk thought—was there no way to gain more time? He looked at the Transporter platform that was to maroon him on Scalos, and Deela said, "Come, Captain. We are leaving your pretty ship. Your crew will be all right. You said so yourself."

He smiled at her. "Know something?" he said. "I think I'll make sure of it." Then he caught her; and wrenching her weapon from her belt, ran for the door.

She screamed into her medallion. "Rael! He broke away! He's armed—"

"I'm ready for him!"

Kirk was racing down the corridor to life support, ducking the stony figures of his crewmen. The beam of a phaser lanced the darkness—and he brought up short. Then he saw Spock. They didn't speak. They didn't need to. A vicious *ping* came from the open life support door. Together, they dodged, split, and, weapons out, plunged through the door.

Rael fired again, missed—and Kirk stunned him with Deela's weapon. At the same moment, Spock's phaser beam struck the Scalosian machine. It continued to flare and throb. Kirk aimed his weapon at it. It burst into flame, melted and was still.

"Nice to see you, Mr. Spock," Kirk said.

"Rael!"

It was Deela. She ran to the slumped body, feeling for its heart. Satisfied, she kissed Rael's lips. Then she looked up at Kirk. "You're very clever, Captain. You tricked me. I should have known you'd never adjust." She had Rael in her arms. "What shall we expect from you?"

"We could put you in suspended animation until we determine how to use you," he said. "What do you want us to do with you?"

She was close to tears. "Oh, Captain, don't make a game of this! We've lost. You've won. Dispose of us."

96

"If I send you back to Scalos, you'll undoubtedly play the same trick on the next space ship that passes."

She was openly weeping now. "There'll never be another one come by. You'll warn them. Your Federation will quarantine this entire aea."

"I'm sure it will."

"And we'll die out. We'll solve your problem that way. And ours."

"Will you accept help?" Kirk said.

"We can't be helped. I've told you . . ."

"Madam," Spock said, "I respectfully suggest that as we are advanced beyond your rating on the Industrial Scale, we may be able to be of some help."

"Our best people in the Federation will work on it. Will you accept our offer, Deela, and go in peace?"

Clearly, there were aspects to Kirk's nature she had not suspected. She looked at him wonderingly. After a moment, the old mischief glinted in her green eyes. She shrugged. "What have we to lose?"

She looked down at Rael. He was recovering consciousness. "We have lost," she told him quietly. "It is you and I who will transport down to Scalos."

He smiled up at her. "Soon," he said.

As they took their places on the platform, Deela turned to Kirk at the console. "Now about your problem, Captain. I note that your Vulcan friend, too, has been accelerated."

Spock spoke. "If you will devote yourself exclusively to the concerns of Scalos, Madam, we shall be very happy to stay and take care of the *Enterprise*."

"Spock," Kirk said, "remind me sometime to tell you how I've missed you."

"Yes, Captain."

"You could find life on Scalos very pleasant, Captain," Deela urged.

"And brief," Kirk said.

"Do I really displease you so much?"

"I can think of nothing I'd like more than staying with you. Except staying alive."

"Will you visit us, Captain?"

"Energize!"

"Captain . . . Captain . . . goodbye . . ."

Spock had moved the controls. They dissolved—and were gone. Kirk stared at the empty platform a long moment. Then, turning briskly to Spock, he said, "And now, how do we get back?"

"Doctor McCoy and I have synthesized a possible counteragent to the Scalosian water, sir. Regrettably, we lacked the opportunity to test it."

"Then let's test it." He took the solution Spock gave him and swallowed it. Deela and Rael. It was all for the best. You couldn't have everything you wanted. Sex—a peculiar magnetic field. Her eyes . . . like wet green leaves . . .

Preoccupied, he vaguely heard Spock say, "Your motion seems to be slowing down, sir."

Kirk started to speak. "Missssterrr . . . Spock!" He drew a deep breath. The counteragent had worked. They were back in their own time! Then, abruptly, he realized that Spock hadn't answered. He wheeled—and before his eyes, Spock vanished.

"Spock! Spock, where are you?"

Scott came through the door to halt in midstride. "*Captain Kirk!*" he yelled. "Where in blazes did you come from?"

There was no cause to panic. Bones would have more of the counteragent. But Vulcan physiology was a tricky thing. What had worked for him would not necessarily work for Spock. What then? A permanent isolation in an accelerated universe? Kirk had whipped out his communicator before he remembered it was useless, dead as the ship itself. The bridge! He had to get to the bridge! Search parties? Futile. They couldn't see him. If Spock were there beside him, he, Kirk himself, couldn't see him.

He ignored the bridge's hubbub of welcome. Passing Uhura's station, he snapped, "Lieutenant, try to set our recorder at maximum speed . . ."

"Yes, sir." But the lights on her console had gone mad. The rapidity of their flashing turned them into blur. And all around him other boards and panels were affected by the same dementia. Suddenly, relief engulfed him. Grinning, he spoke to Scott. "I think we've found Mr. Spock. Lieutenant Uhura, are your circuits clearing?"

Her face was startled. "Yes, sir."

"Mr. Sulu?"

"Clearing, sir."

"Lieutenant Uhura, open all channels." He seized his mike. "Captain to crew. Repairs to the ship are being complated by Mr. Spock. We will resume normal operations . . . just about immediately."

The air beside his chair seemed to thicken. It solidified. Kirk looked at the elegantly pointed ears. "Greetings, Mr. Spock. My compliments on your repair work."

"Thank you, Captain. I have found it all a most fascinating experience."

"I'm glad," Kirk said. "I'm glad on many counts." He got up to pace the round of the stations. "Malfunctions—any anywhere?" Faces beamed at him. He returned to his chair—and the viewing screen lit up. On it the five Scalosians came back into view, Deela's surpassing loveliness transcendent.

"Sorry, sir," Uhura said. "I touched the tape button accidentally."

He leaned back in his chair, eyes on the screen. Deela's face seemed to fill the world. The magnetic field between them—and susceptible to no analysis. The images winked off, leaving the screen blank.

"Goodbye, Deela," he said softly.

Bread and Circuses

(Gene Roddenberry and Gene L. Coon)

There was no doubt about it. The space debris spotted by the *Enterprise* scanners was all that was left of the *Beagle,* an S.S. survey vessel posted as missing for six years. A mixture of personal belongings and portions of instrumentation, the floating junk contained no evidence of human bodies. The conclusion was plain to Kirk. The *Beagle*'s crew had managed to beam down to a planet before catastrophe had destroyed their ship.

"Mr. Chekov," he said, "compute present drift of the wreckage."

"Computed and on the board, sir."

Kirk glanced at the figures. Then he rose and went to his Science officer. "Mr. Spock, assuming that stuff has been drifting at the same speed and direction for six years . . . ?"

Spock completed a reading on his library computer. "It would have come from planet four in Star System eight nine two, directly ahead, Captain."

Chekov called. "Only one-sixteenth parsec away, sir. We could be there in seconds!"

Kirk nodded to him. "Standard orbit around the planet. There may be survivors there, Mr. Chekov."

Spock had more information on the lost *Beagle*. "She was a small Class Four stardrive vessel, crew of forty-seven, commanded by—" He withdrew his head from his hooded viewer. "I believe you know him, sir. Captain R. M. Merrick."

"Yes, at the Academy." It had been a long time ago; and it wasn't too pleasant a memory at that. Merrick had been dropped in his fifth year. Rumor had it he'd gone into the merchant service. True or false, he'd known him. If, by some chance, Merrick was down there, abandoned on that star . . .

Kirk turned to the brige screen. They were coming up on the planet. The pinpoint of light it had been was enlarging, growing rounder, transforming itself into a bluish ball, not unlike Earth. But the oceans and land masses were different.

He said so and Spock shook his head. "In shape only, Captain. The proportion of land to water is exactly as on your home planet. Density 5.5 . . . diameter 7917 at the equator . . . atmosphere 78% nitrogen, 21% oxygen. Again, exactly like Earth." He looked up, gesturing to his viewer-computer. "And I picked up indications of large cities."

"Development?" Kirk said.

"No signs of atomic energy yet. But far enough along for radio communications, power transportation, an excellent road system."

Uhura slewed around from her station. "Captain! I think I can pick up something visual! A 'news broadcast' using a system I believe was once called 'video'."

" 'Television' was the colloquial word," Spock observed.

"Put it on the screen, Lieutenant," Kirk said.

For a moment the bridge viewer held only the picture of the planet at orbital distance. Then, as Uhura made a new adjustment, the pciture dissolved into the image of a city street—one that, apart from some subtle differences, could have been a city street of Earth's 1960's. Clearly a newscast, the scene showed onlookers in clothes of the period watching police herd up a small group of people in loin cloths.

An announcer's voice, filtered, spoke from the screen. ". . . and in the Forum District today, police rounded up still another collection of dissidents. Authorities are as yet unable to explain these fresh outbreaks of treasonable disobediences by well-treated, well-protected slaves . . ."

A shocked, amazed silence fell over the *Enterprise* bridge. But the bland announcer-voice went on. "And now, turning to the world of sports, we bring you taped reports of the arena games last night . . ."

Two men appeared on the Starship's screen. They were naked except for leather aprons. Helmeted, carrying oblong shields, they were armed with ancient Roman swords. They advanced toward each other. One attacked —and the announcer's voice said, "The first heat involved amateurs, a pair of petty thieves from city prison. Conducted, however, with traditional weapons, it provided some amusement for a few moments . . ."

The attacker saw his chance. He lunged, driving his sword into the heart of his opponent. To a background of noisy cheers, he stepped back from the bloody body, raising his sword in salute to the arena's galleries. Over the cheers, the announcer said, "The winner will meet another contestant in tonight's games. In the second heat we'll have a more professional display in the spirit of our splendid past, when gladiator Claudius Marcus killed the last of the barbarians, William B. Harrison, in an excellent example of . . ."

Static crashed. The picture faded to be replaced by the planet view.

An appalled Uhura, collecting herself, said, "Transmission lost, Captain. Shall I try to get it back?"

Kirk didn't answer. Instead, both puzzled and astounded, he turned to Spock. "Slaves and gladiators? Some kind of Twentieth-century Rome?"

Spock's face was unusually grave as he lifted it from his computer. "Captain, the man described as the 'barbarian' is also listed here—Flight Officer William B. Harrison of the S.S. *Beagle*. At least there *were* survivors down there."

A landing party. There was no alternative. Kirk wheeled. "Ready the Transporter Room, Mr. Sulu."

They arrived at the base of a shallow canyon. Glancing up at the rocky overhang, Kirk said, "You could have selected a more attractive place, Mr. Spock."

His first officer was already taking tricorder readings. "Practical, however, Captain. Unpopulated but close to that city we saw. We should not be observed." He looked up from his instrument. "Fascinating how similar is this atmosphere to your Twentieth century's! Moderately industrialized pollution containing substantial amounts of carbon monoxide and partially consumed hydrocarbons."

McCoy said, "The word was 'smog'."

"I believe that *was* the term, Doctor. I had no idea you were such a historian."

"I'm not. I just wanted to stop you before we got the whole lecture. Jim, do we know anything at all about this planet?"

Kirk shook his head. "The *Beagle* was doing the first survey on this star sector when it disappeared."

"Then the 'prime directive' is in full effect, Captain."

"Yes, Mr. Spock. 'No identification of self or mission: no interference with social development of said planet'."

McCoy nodded ruefully. "No references to space, to other worlds or more advanced civilizations." He grinned. "Once, just once, I'd like to land someplace and say, 'Behold, I am the Archangel Gabriel' . . ."

Spock cocked a brow at Kirk's chuckle. "I fail to see any humor in such a masquerade."

McCoy eyed him. "I guess because you could hardly claim to be an angel. But with those ears, Spock, if you landed somewhere carrying a *pitchfork* . . ."

A rifle cracked. Its bullet kicked up the dust at Kirk's feet—and a male voice said, "Don't move! Hands in the air!"

"Complete Earth parallel," Spock remarked. "The language here is English . . ."

The second shot struck close to his feet.

"I said don't move!" the voice shouted.

"I think he means it, Mr. Spock," Kirk said.

Spock looked down at the bullet mark. "That would seem to be evident, sir."

They raised their hands. Above their heads, gravel scuffed to the sound of approaching feet. A big, burly man leaped down from the overhang. Three other men followed him. All wore ragged "slave" loincloths and the alert look of fugitives. Though their rifles were conventionally old-fashioned, they used them skilfully to cover the *Enterprise* trio. Their uniforms seemed to anger the big man. He glared at them with hostility and suspicion.

"Who are you?" he said.

Kirk spoke. "We come from another—'province'."

The man was staring at Spock's ears. "Where are *you* from? Are those ears?"

"I call them ears," Spock told him mildly.

"Are you trying to be funny?"

"Never," Spock assured him. He spoke to Kirk. "Colloquial Twentieth-century English. Truly an *amazing* parallel."

Their captor was clearly baffled. Kirk undertook to enlighten him. "We come from a place quite a distance from here. I doubt if you've ever heard—"

He was interrupted. Pointing to their clothing, the big leader turned to his men. "Uniforms. Probably some new Praetorian Guard unit." His eyes went back to Kirk. "I should kill you here and now . . . but Septimus would probably be displeased. You can take your hands down. Our rifles are at your backs. Move on!" He gestured ahead of them.

They obeyed. After about twenty minutes of hard slugging over the rocky terrain, a man in a tattered loincloth stepped from behind a boulder, rifle at the ready.

"Praetorian spies," the big man told him. "I'm taking them to Septimus."

They were prodded through an entrance of a cave. In its dimness they saw that it held a number of people, the men loinclothed, the women in coarse tunics. At sight of the strangers, they all gathered around an elderly man. Under his gray hair, his features were distinguished and benign.

"I didn't harm them, Septimus," the big man said. "Much as I wanted to."

He received a quiet nod of approval. "Keep always in your mind, Flavius, that our way is peace."

McCoy spoke. "For which we are grateful. We are men of peace ourselves."

105

"Ah? Are you also children of the sun?"

McCoy hesitated. "If you mean a worship of some sort, we represent many beliefs . . ."

"There is only one true belief!" Flavius shouted. "They are Roman butchers sent by the First Citizen!"

Kirk addressed him directly. "Are we like any Roman you ever saw?"

"Then are you slaves like ourselves?" Septimus asked.

"No. Our people do not believe in slavery."

Flavius cried, "A Roman lie! We must kill them, Septimus!"

Spock stepped forward. "Sir, we have come here looking for some friends. Forty-seven of them who . . ." he paused, the "prime directive" in mind . . . "were 'stranded' here six years ago. They wore clothing similar to ours. Have you heard of such men?"

Nobody had. Flavius, still suspicious, said, "Septimus, I know killing is evil but sometimes it's necessary!"

"No."

"They've located our hiding-place! It's better that a few of them die than all of us!"

One of Flavius' men spoke up. "He's right, Septimus. I don't care for myself, but I've brought my wife here, too, my children . . ."

"If they don't die, Septimus, it's the same as if you killed us all yourself!"

Flavius rallied more shouts of agreement. Kirk could see that Septimus was wavering. Rifles were lifting. "Wait," he said. "I can prove we're telling the truth! A small device, Flavius. I'll bring it out slowly . . ."

Fingers were on triggers as he carefully reached for his communicator. He held it out so that it could be openly seen. Then, very slowly, he opened it and placed it to his lips. "Kirk to *Enterprise*. Come in . . ."

Scott's filtered voice was audible in the cave's sudden silence. "Scott here, Captain."

"Lock in on my transmission. Scan us."

"Scanning, sir."

"Including ourselves, how many people in this cave?"

"Twelve, Captain."

Flavius and Septimus looked quickly around, counting. There were indeed twelve people in the cave. Astonished, they looked at Kirk. He smiled at them.

"Maintain scanning, Scotty: we'll continue checking in. Kirk out." He closed the communicator, turning to Septimus. "The *Enterprise* is our vessel . . . sailing out at sea. The voice belongs to one of my crew. That's all I can tell you. If it's not sufficient, then I suppose you'll have to kill us."

Rifles were lowering. Septimus, impressed, spoke to Flavius. "Tell me the Empire has an instrument like that —and you can kill them. Otherwise, accept them as friends."

The tension subsided. A woman came forward, offering a pannikin of milk to Kirk. He smiled at her, drank it and seized his first chance to take in the cave. The beds of the truant slaves were rough-hewn rock ledges. What furniture their retreat contained was equally primitive, battered pots and pans—the crude necessities of their harsh existence. Yet the *Enterprise* men were beginning to feel at ease in the cave. Perhaps it was due to the abruptly warm friendliness of the people's effort to make amends for their original reception of the guests.

It was difficult to credit the way they lived to their era. Telecasts—and that rough log table with its torn magazines and newspapers. Was this star a strange example of Hodgkins Law of parallel planet development? A world much like his own back in the Twentieth century—that was undeniable. But on this odd "Earth," Rome never fell. It survived; and was apparently ruled by emperors who could trace their line back to the Caesars of two thousand years ago.

The fate of the *Beagle* crew uppermost in his mind, Kirk approached Septimus again. But the old man shook his head. "No, Captain. I'm sure I would have heard of the arrival of other men like you."

Kirk persisted. "Have you heard . . . let's say, an impossible story about men coming from the sky? Or from other worlds?"

Septimus smiled. "There are no other worlds."

"The stars . . ."

"Lights shining through from heaven. It is where the sun is. Blessed be the sun."

"Yes, of course. Excuse me . . ."

Spock, holding a magazine, had beckoned. It was titled *The Gallian*; and its cover was the photograph of a gladiator, fully armed with sword, shield, breastplate and helmet. The caption under the picture read, THE NEW HEAVYWEIGHT CHAMPION.

Kirk, leafing through it, came on a colored drawing of a sleek automobile. The ad copy told him its name and purpose. It said: THE JUPITER EIGHT FOR ROYAL COMFORT.

"Fascinating," Spock said.

"The Jupiter Eight. Conventional combustion engine . . . you were right about that smog, Spock. But Jupiter cars? And here's Mars Toothpaste . . . Neptune Bath Salts . . ."

"Taken from the names of false gods," Septimus said. "When I was a Senator, I worshiped them, too . . . but I heard the words of the Sun. I became a brother. For that they made me a slave."

"Septimus . . . will you help us?" Kirk said. "We must go into the city. We know that one of our missing friends was seen there recently . . ."

"My advice to you is to leave this place . . . to go back where you came from."

"We can't do that. Perhaps you have heard this name. 'Merrick' or 'Captain Merrick'?"

Septimus backed away, his face changing. Kirk was suddenly aware of Flavius' watchful eyes.

"Merikus?" Septimus said.

"Merrick. The leader of our friends . . ."

"Merikus is First Citizen!" Flavius cried. "Butcher!"

"It could not be the same man," Kirk told him. "Captain Merrick is no butcher."

Spock interposed. "A logical question if I may, Captain." He addressed Septimus. "How many years ago did this Merikus become First Citizen?"

"Perhaps five years . . ."

"Almost six!" Flavius was openly hostile now. "I was there when he became Lord of the Games! If he is your friend, you are no friends of ours!"

Kirk thought fast. "Septimus, it is one of our most important laws that none of us may interfere in the affairs of

108

others. If Merrick is Merikus, he is in violation of that law! He will be taken away and punished. Help us find out the truth of this!"

"I must discuss it with the others," Septimus said. Beckoning to Flavius, he moved away to his people, leaving the *Enterprise* men alone.

Spock said, "Curious, Captain. The similarity of the names. Were you told why Merrick was dropped from the Space Academy?"

"He failed a psycho-simulator test. All it takes is a split second of indecision." He shook his head. "Hardly the kind who becomes a strongman butcher."

"Odd that these people worship the sun," McCoy said.

"Why, Doctor?"

"Because, my dear Spock, it's *illogical*. Rome had no sun worshipers. Why would they parallel Rome in every way but that?"

"Hold it," Kirk said. He had seen Septimus and Flavius returning.

"We have decided," the old man announced. "Flavius will guide you. We will provide you with suitable clothing. But I caution you—take great care. The police are everywhere. May the blessings of the sun be upon you."

A woman shyly approached Spock, a worn scarf in her hand. He understood. Stooping, he waited until she had bound it around his ears.

The outskirts of the city made good ambush country, rough, wooded, brushy. At a thick copse of low-branched trees, Flavius signaled for a halt. "We wait here until dark," he said. "The police seek everywhere."

"Were you a slave, too, Flavius?" Kirk asked.

The big man straightened proudly. "You are barbarians, indeed, not to know of Flavius Maximus. For seven years, I was the most successful gladiator in the province."

"Then you heard the word of the sun?"

"Yes. The words of peace and freedom. It was not easy for me to believe. I was trained to fight. But the words were true."

"There are many other things I would—" Kirk broke

off as the ex-gladiator held up his hand, alarm leaping into his face. "Quickly . . ."

"Hold! Don't move! Hands in the air!"

There was a warning rattle of machine-gun fire. Bullets tore leaves from the trees. A half-dozen policemen broke from cover, all armed with oddly-shaped submachine guns. Yet, topping their uniforms were Roman helmets, and at the waist of each hung a short Roman sword. Their leader stepped in close, his hard face cold. "Four fleeing fish! A fine haul—" He stopped. Staring at Flavius, he shouted, "By all the gods, Flavius Maximus!"

With a muffled oath, Flavius lunged at him. One of the others struck him down with the butt of his gun. The *Enterprise* men, directly under the guns, were unable to move. The hard-jawed leader grinned as he looked down at Flavius. "You have been too long absent from the games," he said. "The First Citizen will be pleased."

He nodded his head toward the Starship three. His men shook them down, removing their phasers, communicators, Spock's tricorder and McCoy's medikit.

"What are these things?" he demanded.

Kirk shook his head slightly, signaling silence. The policeman took another curious look at the equipment. Then, shaking his head, he said, "No matter. Escaped slaves are welcome, whatever the circumstances." Spock's head scarf caught his eye. He ripped it off. For a moment, he stared at the Vulcan ears in wonder. He shrugged the wonder off.

"Not escaped slaves," he said. "Barbarians. A good day's work. It's a long time since I watched barbarians die in the arena."

Apparently, the arena's vestibule was a jail's cell. Shoved into one, Kirk's first act was to shake its bars. The policeman outside struck his hands away from them, cutting his knuckles. But Kirk had succeeded in attracting special attention. "Tell Merikus we want to see him," he told the man.

"The First Citizen? Why would he bother with arena bait like you?"

"Tell him it's James Kirk. Perhaps a friend of his."

The man laughed. " 'Perhaps' is right."

"Suppose I *am* a friend and you didn't tell him? Do you really care to risk that?"

He received a glare, a grunt—and the policeman walked off to join his men.

Time ambled by. Kirk watched McCoy doing what was possible for Flavius' head gash. When the wound had stopped bleeding, he said, "Tell me, Flavius. If there have been slaves for over two thousand years, haven't there always been discontents, runaways?"

Flavius sat up. "Long ago there were rebellions. But they were suppressed. And with each century the slaves acquired more rights under the law. They received the right to medicine, to government payments in their old age." He shrugged. "They finally learned to be content."

Spock looked up from a stone bench. "Yet more fascinating. Slavery evolving into guaranteed medical care, old age pensions . . ."

"Quite logical, I'd say, Mr. Spock," McCoy said. "Just as it's logical that a Twentieth-century Rome would use television to show its gladiator contests, or name a new car the Jupiter Eight or—"

Spock interrupted. "Were I able to show emotion, Doctor, your new infatuation with the term 'logical' would begin to annoy me."

"Medical men are trained in logic, Mr. Spock!"

"Your pardon, Doctor. I had no idea they were trained. From watching you I assumed it was trial and error."

Flavius eyed them. "Are they enemies, Captain?"

Kirk smiled. "I'm not sure they're sure." He returned to the absorbing subject of this extraordinary half-Rome place. "But, Flavius, when the slaves began to worship the sun, they became discontented again. When did all this begin?"

"Long ago. Perhaps as long ago as the beginning of the Empire. But the message of the sun was kept from us."

"That all men are brothers?"

Flavius nodded. "Perhaps I'm a fool to believe it. It does often seem that a man must fight to live."

"No," Kirk said. "You go on believing it, Flavius. All men *are* brothers."

Footsteps sounded outside the cell. The wolfish policeman, his men behind him, unlocked the barred door. "Flavius Maximus! Your old friends are waiting for you. You are already matched for the morning games. Come!"

Flavius spoke quietly. "I will not fight. I am a brother of the sun."

A cynical grin lifted the man's lips from his teeth. "Put a sword in your hand—and you'll fight. I know you, Flavius. You're as peaceful as a bull."

His men had their submachine guns. Two of them, flanking Flavius, marched him out of the cell. The police chief, with his two remaining guards, gestured to the others. "You three . . . come with us!"

Kirk, lowering his voice for Spock and McCoy, said, "Three and three. We may never have a better—"

"No talking!" the police chief barked. "Outside now!"

Kirk pointed to McCoy. "I doubt he can walk far. He feels ill."

"I do?" said McCoy.

"He'll die of something if he doesn't step out of this cell right now!"

Kirk's purpose had suddenly dawned on McCoy. He went along with it. "No, I think I can walk. I'll try, anyway . . ."

The three, exchanging glances, silently agreed it was to be now or never.

The guards closed in around them. Halfway down the outside corridor, McCoy moaned, *"Uhhh . . . my stomach . . ."* He doubled up, his knees buckling to heart-rending groans of pain. A guard grabbed him to pull him back upright; and Spock, with a show of assisting the man, managed to get a hand on his shoulder. The guard crumpled under the Vulcan neck pinch. At the same instant Kirk's clenched fist lashed out. It caught the police chief on the button. He spun around and fell. Coming up fast from his crouch, McCoy downed the third man. Two of the guards tried to struggle up. For their pains they got a couple of space karate chops and subsided into unconsciousness.

A voice said, "Well done, Jim."

The *Enterprise* men wheeled.

The door at the corridor's end had opened. Kirk recognized the man standing inside it. It was Merrick. The ex-captain of the S.S. *Beagle* had always been handsome; and passing time had added strength to what had been merely a goodlooking Space Academy cadet. He wore a richly tailored sports jacket and slacks of a princely elegance. Yet, despite the strength and the clothes, Kirk thought he detected a look of haunting tragedy in his eyes. Beside him was a smaller, plump man, softish, also fashionably tailored. They hadn't come alone. Behind them were ranged policemen, all armed with submachine guns.

Merrick said, "But it isn't that easy, Jim. They've been handling slaves for two thousand years."

The smaller man beside him turned. "But it was exciting, Merik. They'd do well in the arena."

Kirk hadn't recovered from the shock of recognition. "Bob Merrick! It is you . . ."

"Me, Merik." He indicated the massed guards behind him. "And them. Not to mention them . . ." He pointed to the opposite end of the corridor. It was crowded with more armed guards.

The smaller man spoke again. "But this is no place for a reunion."

The hand Kirk had known as Bob Merrick's waved them to follow. "This way, Jim . . . your friends, too. Lots to talk about, lots to explain, to—"

Kirk eyed him. "Yes," he said quickly. "I agree."

Merik made an impatient gesture. "Don't judge me without the facts. Come along. We'll be able to talk freely. The Proconsul here knows who and what we are."

They left. And the guards moved in to make sure that the *Enterprise* three followed them.

It was a lush apartment into which the trio was marched. Marble columns supported a ceiling of mosaic that depicted nymphs disporting with satyrs. A fountain of colored water flung its spray up and back into a seashell of marble. Tufted couches of gleaming stuff were arranged about the room, low tables beside them. All four of the chamber's walls bore painted murals of old Roman gods at their pleasures. Young women—slaves chosen and bought for their loveliness—were moving to the tables with gold platters of fruit and sweetmeats.

The plump Proconsul, wine goblet in hand, greeted them. Merik, an easy host in his sleek sports jacket, waved the guards out of the room.

Smiling at Kirk, he said, "This is a personal affair, isn't it, Jim? A celebration. Old friends meeting."

The Proconsul spoke to the slaves. "Wine for our friends. They have come from a great distance, eh, Captain Kirk?" He grinned broadly. "A very great distance. I am Claudius Marcus, Proconsul." He approached Spock. "So this is a Vulcan. Interesting. From what I've heard, I wish I had fifty of you for the arena."

Merik said hastily, "And this other is your ship's surgeon?"

"Dr. McCoy," Kirk said tersely.

Merik spoke to Claudius. "A pity we can't turn him loose in your hospitals. The level of medicine here might benefit."

One of the girls was proffering a tray to Claudius. "You must be hungry," he told Kirk. "Do try the sparrows broiled with garum. Delicious. Or the roast kid." He jerked a thumb toward the girl. "Drusilla. A lovely thing, isn't she? Noticeable."

So he'd been caught staring at her. She was indeed noticeable. Blond hair, dark eyes—and in the violet, peplum-like gown she wore, every movement of her slender body was grace itself. Flushing, Kirk turned to Merik. "What happened to your ship?" he said.

"Meteor damage. I—" A slave was passing and he paused before he said, "I 'came ashore' with a landing party for iridium ore and repairs. Then I met Claudius . . ."

"Go on," Kirk said.

"He convinced me it was unfair to this world to carry word of its existence elsewhere."

"Contamination," Claudius said. "We can't risk that. You'll understand as you learn more about us, Kirk."

"I made . . . the decision to stay," Merik said.

"What happened to your crew? Did they voluntarily beam—" Kirk corrected himself, "—come ashore?"

"This is an ordered world, Jim. Conservative, based on time-honored Roman strengths and virtues."

"What happened to your crew?"

"There has been no war here for over four hundred

years, Jim. Could your land of the same era make the same boast? Certainly, they don't want this stability contaminated with dangerous ideas about other ways and other places."

"Interesting," Spock said. "And given a conservative empire, Captain, quite understandable."

McCoy was horrified. "Spock, are you out of your head?" he demanded.

"Doctor, I said I understood. I find the checks and balances of this civilization quite illuminating. It does seem to have escaped the carnage of your first three World Wars."

"Spock, they have *slavery, despotism, gladiatorial games . . . !*"

Imperturbable as usual, the Vulcan said, "Situations quite familiar to the six million who died in your First World War, Doctor—the eleven million who died in your Second, the thirty-seven million in your Third. Shall I go on?"

"Interesting," Claudius commented. "And you, Captain . . . which world do you prefer?"

"My world," Kirk said, "is my vessel, my oath and my crew, Proconsul." He turned to Merik. "What happened to your vessel, you've answered. What happened to your oath is obvious."

Merik didn't flinch. "As to my men, Kirk, those who can't adapt to a world always die."

The words were called for. Kirk said them. "You sent your own people to the arena." It was a statement, not a question—a statement defining an unbridgeable gulf between life values. Yes, Merik's eyes *were* haunted. And he would be forever pursued by the Furies of his own self-betrayal. If he could still speak with firmness, it was a false firmness—a poor rag clutched around a shivering soul.

"And just as I did, Kirk, you'll end up ordering your own people 'ashore'."

Misery loves company, Kirk thought. McCoy had cried out, "You must know that's impossible! Starfleet regulations—"

Claudius completed the sentence. "—are designed to circumvent any such order. There may be over four hundred people on your ship, Captain, but they'll come

115

down if it's handled properly . . . a few at a time." The plump little man smiled. "You forget I have a trained ship captain to tell me what is possible and what is not possible." He took a communicator from the pocket of his smart sports jacket. "Your communicator, Captain Kirk. Save us all a lot of unnecessary trouble and issue the appropriate orders."

Merik tried for a comradely tone. "They'll be arriving soon anyway, Jim. A recon party first. Then a rescue party, then a larger rescue party. I had less men but it adds up to the same in the end."

Kirk smiled at them. "You really believe I can be made to order my people down?"

"I believe this, Captain," Claudius said. "You'd do almost anything rather than have to watch your two friends here put slowly to death."

The soft little man was anything but soft. The plump body was built on bones of cold steel. Kirk felt the sweat breaking out on his palms. Then he reached out and took the communicator.

"Jim!"

Kirk opened the communicator, ignoring McCoy's cry of protest. "Captain to bridge, come in . . ."

"Bridge, Scott here. Go ahead, sir."

Reaching down, Claudius pressed a button as Kirk spoke quickly into the communicator. "If you have a fix on us, Scotty—" He stopped. The door had opened. Guards' submachine guns were leveled at him, at Spock, at McCoy.

"Stand by, Engineer . . ." Kirk closed the communicator.

"Wise of you, Captain," Claudius said. "No point in beaming up three bullet-ridden corpses."

"On the other hand my chief engineer is standing by for a message. If I bring down a hundred men armed with phasers . . ."

"You could probably defeat the combined armies of our entire empire." Claudius' lips moved in a smile that Kirk was beginning to dread. "At a cost, Captain—the violation of your oath regarding noninterference with other societies." He addressed Spock. "I believe you all swear you'll die before you'll violate that directive. Am I right?"

116

"Quite correct," Spock said.

McCoy's tension exploded. "Spock, must you always be so blasted honest?"

Claudius returned to the workover on Kirk. "Why even bother to bring down armed men? I'm told your vessel can easily lay waste to this world's surface." He smiled once more. "Oh, but there's that prime directive in the way again, isn't there? Mustn't interfere." He pointed to the communicator. "Well, Captain, you've a message started. Your engineer is waiting. What are you going to do?"

This Roman in the sports jacket would have been a priceless asset to the Spanish Inquisition. It was small comfort to know at last what he was up against. Kirk opened the communicator. "Sorry to keep you waiting, Scotty . . ."

Claudius, at his shoulder, heard Scott say, "We were becoming concerned, Captain. You were a bit overdue."

"Order your officers to join us." Claudius said.

" 'Condition green'," Kirk said. "All is well. Captain out." He closed the communicator.

Claudius hurled his wine goblet across the room. He snatched the communicator and Merik shouted, "Jim, that was stupid!"

Claudius was fairly dancing with fury. "Guards, take them! Prepare them for the games!"

As the three were hustled past Merik, the ex-captain said, "This is no Academy training test, Kirk! *This is real! They're taking you out to die!*"

Miles above it all, an unhappy Scott was torn by indecision of his own. "Condition green" was a code term for trouble. But it also forbade the taking of any action to relieve it. Kirk seldom signaled trouble. Now that he *had* signaled it, it would be bad trouble.

Scott left the command chair to go to Uhura. "Lieutenant, are you *certain* there's no contact?"

"Nothing, Mr. Scott. Except for their message you received."

"Mr. Chekov?"

"Nothing, sir. Sensors lost them when they entered the city."

With action immobilized, fancied horrors began to parade themselves for the miserable Scott.

117

The arena was a TV studio sound stage. Somebody had done a good job on his Roman history. The stage was galleried, its tiers of rounded stone benches rising in genuine Colosseum style. But the cameras were focused on the sand-sprinkled central space below where combat was won or lost. At the cameraman's "ready" signal, an announcer assumed the amiable smile that was the twentieth-century's stock-in-trade of announcers the world over.

Canned music blared; and to a red light's flash, the announcer went on the air.

"Good evening, ladies and gentlemen. Live from City Arena tonight and in living color, we bring you 'Name the Winner!' Brought to you by your Jupiter Eight dealers from coast to coast. In a moment, tonight's first heat . . ."

The light read: OFF THE AIR—and the announcer's big smile vanished as though it had never been. There was an Observers' Booth, hung with velvet, behind him. Claudius and Merik were the first to enter it. Armed guards with Kirk, his arms bound behind his back, followed them. The announcer turned. "We're in a taped commercial, Proconsul. Back on the air in forty seconds," he said.

The guards shoved Kirk into a chair, their guns aimed at his back. Merik, his self-assurance visibly less, threw him a concerned glance. But Claudius, fully at home here, merely turned to make sure that Kirk had noted the entrance into the combat space.

Spock and McCoy were standing in it.

Clad in gladiator gear, they'd been given Roman shields and swords. Spock held his weapon with the born athlete's confidence; but McCoy was fingering his awkwardly. Looking up, they both caught sight of Kirk—and he knew that their anxiety for him matched his anxiety for them. But there wasn't time even for anxiety. Horror filled Kirk. To their rear was a man with a rawhide whip: an older man, the Master of the Games, thickly-muscled, his hard face that of a veteran who knew the gladiator racket from the bottom up.

The announcer said, "Stand by . . . ten seconds!"

The older man signed to the pair's guard escort. Pointed swords were pressed against their backs. "If they refuse to move on out, skewer them," the hardbitten veteran told the guards.

118

"Condition green." Maybe it had been a mistake to prohibit action by the *Enterprise*. Kirk hadn't visualized anything like this. He moved in his bonds, straining against them as the announcer got his ON THE AIR light.

"And first tonight, a surprise 'extra'! In the far corner, a couple of aggressive barbarians with strange ways I'm sure will be full of surprises. Facing them, your favorites and mine from previous matches—Maximus Achilles and our noted Flavius!"

Flavius, the experienced gladiator. And the other one, just as big, just as competent-looking. Kirk could estimate their familiarity with the work at hand by the way they were moving out into the arena. Equally efficient, the sports announcer was milking his last ounce of suspense from the spectacle.

"Victory—or death? And for which of them? You know as much as I do at this moment. Ladies and gentlemen, this is *your* program! *You 'Name the Winner'*!"

To the beat of more canned music, the two big gladiators saluted the Proconsul with lifted swords. Then they stepped forward toward Spock and McCoy.

Intuition had placed Spock into a nearly correct defensive stance. McCoy lacked it. Despite his Starship combat training, he wasn't the athletic match of either Spock or the tested fighters who were approaching them.

Nearing them, Flavius said quietly, "Why you? I don't mind killing humans but—"

A flourish of trumpets drowned his words. Maximus, eyeing Spock, chose him for his opponent. The Vulcan pivoted, evading the first sword slash. McCoy found himself confronting Flavius, both of them hesitant, unsure.

The whip cracked. "Begin!"

Always reluctant to take a life, Spock was merely defending himself. Maximus bored in on him. Flavius took a half-hearted slash at McCoy and missed. Instinctively, the *Enterprise* man lifted his weapon—and the contest was under way.

Again, Claudius turned to check on Kirk's reactions. They were extremely satisfactory. The Starship Captain had paled and was sitting unnaturally still, his forehead beaded with sweat. The edgy Merik didn't turn; but the back of his neck was red with shamed blood.

The announcer was saying, "Flavius is getting off to a slow start, but he's never disappointed us for very—*there's a close one! The barbarian with the pointed ears is in trouble!*"

Spock's recoil from offensive action had backed him into a corner, and the huge Maximus was closing in to finish him off.

"Please . . ." Spock said. "I tell you I am well able to defeat you."

"*Fight*, Barbarian!"

Once more Spock barely avoided a sword slash. He was thrown off balance and Maximus raised his weapon to end the match. Watching, Kirk tried to get to his feet. Slammed back by a guard, he felt the cold muzzle of a submachine gun pushed against his neck. Merik leaned back, his voice lowered. "Most of my men went the same way. I'd hoped I'd feel it less with yours . . ."

Pure defense had its disadvantages. In the arena, Spock had dodged another slash only to expose himself to another one. "I *beg* you . . . I don't want to . . ." He ducked again. ". . . injure you . . ."

The cords binding Kirk's arms were slippery with sweat. Every muscle in his body revolted against his helplessness. They were his for action—action he'd taken time and again when Spock needed action. His face reflected his agony. Claudius, turning once more, found it more interesting than his games.

Their Master was displeased. "*Fight, you two!*" He crashed his whip hard across Flavius' naked back. The gladiator's sword came up. Then it dropped, as experience warned him that the old survivor of hundreds of bloody bouts was far too canny to ever blunder into weapon reach.

"You bring this network's ratings down, Flavius—and we'll do a 'special' on you . . ."

The oldtimer's threat worked. Flavius aimed a more skillful blow at McCoy, the massive power of his right arm evident even at half-strength. McCoy staggered back.

"Merik . . ." Kirk said.

Claudius spoke. "Question, Captain?"

"The rules?" Kirk said. "If Spock should finish his man first . . ."

Claudius shook his head. "He can't help his friend.

120

We believe that men should fight their own battles." He smiled his dreadful soft smile again. "Ready to order your crew down? Only the weak will die. My word as a Roman, Captain."

"No," Kirk said.

His tension was beginning to affect Merik. The one-time Space Academy cadet checked Claudius; and leaning back to Kirk said very quietly, "Maybe . . . you understand now why I gave in, Jim. Romans were always the strongest . . . two thousand years practice enslaving people, using them, killing them . . ."

Claudius had overheard. Without turning, he said, "Quite true, Captain Kirk." He pointed to the arena. "The games have always strengthened us. Death becomes familiar. We don't fear it as you do. Admit it . . . you find these games frightening, repellent . . ."

"Frightening." Should he say, "Your games don't frighten me. The spirit behind them does." The little man wanted fear. Kirk wasn't giving him any. "In some parts of the galaxy," he said, "I've seen forms of entertainment that make this look like a folkdance."

It hit home. For the first time, Claudius eyed him with uncertainty.

The whip had again cracked across Flavius' back. Boos came from the guards and galleries. Irritated, the huge gladiator snarled, "At least defend yourself!"

McCoy, angered, too, cried, "I *am* defending myself!"

"Not like that, you fool! Hold your weapon higher! *Now, swing at me!*"

McCoy swung, almost losing his balance. Flavius diverted the blow with an easy wrist movement. McCoy's anger mounted with his realization of his own incompetence. And Flavius, smarting under the lashings, the continuing jeers, was struggling with a growing rage of his own.

The wet cords that held Kirk should have been easier to slip out of. His hands were wrenching at them when he saw that Claudius was watching him. He stopped struggling; and Claudius said, "Those are *your* men dying down there, Captain, not strangers."

Kirk's eyes met his. "I've had to select men to die before, Proconsul, so that more could be saved."

121

"You're a clever liar." There was a pause before the little Twentieth-century Roman gestured to the man beside him. "He was a space captain, too. I've examined him thoroughly. Your species has no strength."

Kirk didn't answer. Merik shifted uneasily; and Claudius, noticing his move, snapped, "Well, what is it? *Out with it!*"

"He . . . Jim . . . Kirk commands not just a space ship, Proconsul, but a *Starship*." Merik flushed under Claudius' glare. "A special kind of vessel . . . and crew. I tried for such a command but . . ." His words trailed off into silence.

Claudius looked down at Spock and McCoy. "I see no evidence of superiority. They fight no better than your men, Merikus. Perhaps not as well."

And indeed the galleries' hissing was growing in volume. *"Stop running!"* Maximus yelled at Spock. *"Fight!"*

He stabbed at him; and Spock, deftly turning the blow, threw a quick look toward McCoy. Then he maneuvered his fight closer to McCoy and Flavius.

"Do you need help, Doctor?"

Frustrated and furious, McCoy shouted, "Whatever gave you *that* idea?" He made another swing at Flavius; and Maximus, maddened by Spock's elusiveness, bellowed, *"Fight,* you pointed-eared freak!"

"You tell him, Buster!" McCoy told Maximus. He tried for a better grip on his sword. *"Of course*, I need help! Of all . . ." Enraged at Spock, McCoy went into a flurry of wild lunges at Flavius, unaware that he was rousing a blood-madness that would turn his antagonist into a very formidable enemy. ". . . the illogical, completely ridiculous questions I ever heard," he panted. He swung again.

Flavius growled deep in his throat. He charged with a series of murderous slashes that snapped McCoy back into reality—the fact that he'd provoked a savagery which could put an end to his life in a matter of seconds.

Spock recognized his sudden peril. He went into his first attack, amazing the towering Maximus by his speed and efficiency. He streaked in on the gladiator, closer and closer; but McCoy was already beaten down to the sand, his shield torn from his grasp. He'd learned enough to parry the next blow. Then his sword was wrenched from his hand.

Kirk saw how defenseless he was. He pulled himself away from the guns behind him and got to his feet, surging against his bonds. They held: and the guards, slamming him back into his seat, immobilized him.

Spock, downing his man with a "space karate" chop, was racing across the arena. He reached Flavius; and spinning him around, dropped him with his Vulcan neck pinch. The arena went into bedlam. The Master of the Games rushed to the *Enterprise* men to cries of "Foul!" from the galleries. His guards, running after him, grabbed both Spock and McCoy and pinioned their arms behind their backs.

Kirk, Claudius and Merik were all on their feet.

The shocked announcer whirled to Claudius. "A clear foul, Proconsul! Your decision?"

Down in the arena, swords were pointed, pressing, against the captives' necks. The Master of the Games looked up to the Observers' Booth for the Proconsul's word, ignoring the galleries' clamor for immediate death. Claudius spoke to Merik.

"Your opinion, Merikus? After all they're like yourself."

Whatever his opinion was, Merik considered it safer to keep it to himself. "It . . . it's *your* decision, Proconsul."

Claudius turned. "And *your* opinion, Captain Kirk?" He didn't wait to hear it. "Kill them now—and you'll gladly accept whatever happens to you. I wouldn't relish that —but you almost tricked me into depriving myself of real pleasure." He moved to the edge of the booth. "Master of the Games, take them back to their cage!"

He turned again to face Kirk. "It won't be easy for them, Captain. And especially not for you!" He spoke to Kirk's guards. "Bring him to my quarters. *Now!*"

He left the booth. And the guards hustled Kirk along after him.

After the raw violence of the arena, the effete luxury of Claudius' suite sickened Kirk. It was the triumph of an art connoisseur. The room was tapestried; and an alcove held a wide bed embroidered in gold. In a large wall niche, a marble statue of Minerva, Roman goddess of wisdom, presided over those self-indulgences that were the delectation of the soft man of steel.

The guards marched Kirk into the room and left him. There was no one in sight. But Claudius had promised that something particularly unpleasant was going to happen to him here. Wary, uncertain, Kirk searched the room with his eyes. A heavy Etruscan jar stood on a pedestal. Kirk seized it, hefting it for weight and balance. If he was going to die, he wasn't going to do it without a fight . . .

"I was told . . ."

It was a feminine voice. Drusilla moved out from the bed alcove's hangings, hesitating at the sight of Kirk with his lifted weapon. This time the gown she wore was pure white. Her straight blond hair fell below her waist. And the white of her gown enhanced the creamy tone of her skin.

"I was told," she said, "to wait for you." She went to a table. "And to provide wine, food, whatever you wish. I am the Proconsul's slave, although for this evening . . ." She was pouring wine, clearly expecting him to come to the table. He didn't move. Inevitably what occurred in this room was bound to lead to treachery, torture and in the end, to certain death.

She turned, surprised by his stillness. "I was told that for this evening, I am *your* slave. Then command me."

"No," Kirk said. "You can tell the Proconsul it won't work."

She frowned, puzzled. "What will not work?"

"Whatever he has in mind. Whatever trickery or . . ."

She left the table to lay a hand on his arm. This master of hers, though temporary, obviously required soothing. Kirk removed the hand. Then he shouted, *"Do you hear me, Proconsul?* Whatever you have in mind, I'm not cooperating! I may have to die—but I won't give you entertainment out of it!"

Drusilla came closer to him but, brushing her roughly aside, he strode past her to the door. He opened it, looking into the corridor, sure he'd find a spy lurking in it. It was empty. He and the slave girl seemed to be totally alone.

She divined his thought. "Except for the guards at the

124

street entrances, we are alone here," she said. "Please believe me. I have never lied to one who owns me."

But Kirk's suspicion wasn't laid. This *had* to be a grotesque trick of some new variety . . . and yet the girl's every word and gesture spoke of sincerity. She seemed honestly puzzled by his behavior—and in her extremely feminine way, a little disappointed by it, too.

He began to wish he could relax. His friends' lives had been spared—but to what purpose? What was going on in that "cage" where they'd been confined?

Going on in the cage was determined escape effort. Its door was barred; and Spock, rallying every ounce of his strength, was trying to pull it loose by the very fury of the need to do so. McCoy, standing behind him, saw that neither bars nor door had given a half-inch.

"Angry, Spock? Or frustrated, perhaps?"

"Such emotion is quite foreign to me, Doctor. I was merely testing the strength of the door."

McCoy nodded. "For the fifteenth time."

Spock came close to showing irritation. Disdaining to answer, he turned from the door, again inspecting the cell for some possible weapon or escape route. Watching him, McCoy's eyes softened. After a space, he said gently, "Spock . . ."

Spock turned, expecting a jibe for what was clearly his frantic anxiety for the safety of his captain. And though McCoy shared it, he had another matter on his mind at the moment.

"Spock, uh . . . we've had our disagreements . . ." Because he was leveling, he was deeply embarrassed. ". . . or maybe they're jokes. As Jim says, we're often not sure ourselves. But . . . er . . . what I mean to say is . . ." He hesitated again. "Well, what I mean is—"

"Doctor," Spock said, "I'm seeking a weapon or an escape method. Please be brief."

"I'm . . . trying to say you saved my life in the arena."

Spock nodded. "Quite true."

That fact mutually acknowledged, he resumed his examination of every possibility of their cell.

McCoy blew up. *"I was trying to thank you, you—you pointed-eared hobgoblin!"*

"Ah, yes," Spock said. "Humans do suffer from an emotional need to show gratitude." He gave a small nod. " 'You're welcome' is, I believe, the correct response." He moved off, still searching. "However, Doctor, you should remember that I am motivated solely by logic. The loss of our ship's surgeon, whatever I may think of his relative skill, is a loss to the efficiency of our vessel and therefore to—"

McCoy interrupted. "Do you know why you're not afraid of dying, Spock? *You're more afraid of living.* Every day you stay alive is one more day you might slip—and let your human half peek out." He lessened the distance between them. "That's it, isn't it? *Insecurity!* You wouldn't know what to do with a genuine, warm, decent feeling!"

Spock wheeled—and this time McCoy caught him at it. There was an instant when he actually saw Spock composing his face into Vulcan impassivity. Then the instant was gone—and Spock raised an eyebrow.

"Really, Doctor?" he said.

McCoy thought, "I am very fond of this man." What he said was, "I know. I'm worried about Jim, too, Spock."

For the moment, anyway, their captain was safe. He was also hungry. And seated beside Drusilla on a couch, he was making excellent inroads on the tray of food she insisted on holding for him. It was a long time since he's tasted roast pheasant. And the wine was good wine. After all, food was food and wine was wine, unlikely to be up to tricks. As to the girl . . . Hunger and thirst appeased, he took his first good look at her.

"You've noticed me at last," she said. "I was becoming concerned. I am ordered to please you."

Kirk sipped more wine. "Good," he said. Then he pointed to the roast pheasant's remains. "Excellent. And you?"

"Superb, I'm told," she said, straight-faced. "But then, men lie, don't they?"

Kirk eyed her. Then he leaned back against the couch. "I've seen strange worlds, strange customs," he told her. "Perhaps here this is considered torture."

She moved close to him, placing the tray on the table. "Torture? I do not understand. I have no wish to see you tortured in any way." She kissed him. "At the first sign of pain, you will tell me?"

"You'll be the first to know," he said. He took her in his arms and returned the kiss with interest.

Up on the *Enterprise,* Scott was tiring of misery. He was rapidly transforming it into the kind of productive anger that opens up new vistas for action.

"How long since we've heard?" he asked Uhura.

"Nine hours, forty-one seconds, sir." She indicated the viewivg screen. "It's almost dark there. We'll see the city lights coming on soon."

"Mr. Chekov, take over the scanners. Lieutenant Uhura, give him a hand." He returned to the command chair, still hesitating. On the other hand, no order had said he couldn't frighten whoever it was down there who was causing bad trouble for his captain and the landing party. It might do no good. Yet it just could be salutary to suggest what a Starship could really do if it got serious.

He made up his mind. "Lieutenant Uhura, pinpoint the city's power source locations." He paused before he added, "Mr. Chekov, type the power, the load factors— and how much our beams must pull to overload them."

"Captain . . ."

Sprawled in sleep on the alcove's bed, Kirk came instantly awake at the sound of Claudius' voice. He had started to roll, protecting himself when he saw that the little man was alone, just standing there, a newly benign look on his face.

"You've had a harrowing time on our planet," he said. "I'm not surprised you slept through the afternoon." He left the alcove to go to a table. "Sorry I was detained. Shall we have our talk now?"

He was pouring wine. Kirk followed him, distrust rising again at sight of the armed guard posted just outside the door. Offered wine, he shook his head. Claudius went on. "Oh, one of the communicators we took from you is missing. Was it my pretty Drusilla by any chance?"

Kirk didn't answer. Merik had entered the room.

Claudius, pointing to Kirk, said, "See if he has the communicator."

Still silent, Kirk permitted the search. "Not that I would have punished him badly. I would have blamed you, Merik," Claudius said. He lifted his goblet. "You're a Roman, Kirk—or should have been. It's not on his person?"

"No, Proconsul." Merik addressed Kirk. "He said a 'Roman.' You've just received as great a compliment, Jim—"

Claudius interrupted. "Care for food, Captain Kirk?"

Kirk saw that Merik, pointedly uninvited to sit, was shifting uncomfortably. "Thank you, I've eaten," he said.

"I trust there was nothing you required that you didn't receive," Claudius said.

"Nothing. Except . . . perhaps an explanation."

"I'm sure our world seems as strange to you as yours would seem to me." He looked up. "Since you are a man, I owe you this immediately. You must die in a few hours." He swallowed. "And also because you are a man . . ." He became conscious of Merik's presence and a flicker of something like contempt passed across his face. "You may leave us, Merik. The thoughts of one man shared with another cannot interest you."

Merik almost responded to the open insult. Then he decided that for him silence was golden. He left the room; and Claudius, resuming. said to Kirk, "And since you are a man, Captain Kirk, I gave you some last hours as a man. Do you understand?"

A small smile on his lips, Kirk said, "Let's say . . . I appreciated it."

"Unfortunately, your defiances in the arena were seen by the television audience. We must demonstrate that defiance is wrong."

"Of course," Kirk said.

"But because I have learned to respect you, I promise you will die quickly and easily."

"Naturally, I prefer that. And my friends?"

"Of course, you'd ask that. And, of course, when their time comes, the same." Summoning guards, he gestured to Kirk. "Take him to the arena." A comforting afterthought occurred to him. "We've preempted fifteen minutes on the early show for you," he told Kirk. "We will have a good

128

audience, full color. You may not understand the honor, since you are centuries beyond anything as crude as television."

"I recall it was similar," Kirk said.

They hadn't bound his hands. He needed them to hold his sword and shield. From the arena's entrance, where Spock and McCoy had waited, he would see Claudius moving into the Observers' Booth above him. Guards, supervised by the Master of the Games, pushed him past a big man in gladiator dress. He recognized Flavius. The two were exchanging glances when Merik's voice, speaking to one of the guards, said, "I'll speak privately with the prisoner."

The Master of the Games was annoyed. "Impossible," he said shortly.

"*I am still First Citizen. You will obey me!*"

The announcer spoke. "Stand by . . . ten seconds."

The Master of the Games, completely ignoring Merik, moved Kirk out into the arena's center. Desperate, the man who'd betrayed himself, shouted, "Too late to help you, Jim! I'll do what I can for your friends!"

The announcer, on signal, was speaking into his microphone. "Good evening, ladies and gentlemen. Before the first heat tonight, a simple execution. But keep your dial turned to this channel—there's lots of excitement to follow . . ."

Claudius leaned over the booth's edge. "Master of the Games, make it quick! A single thrust!"

The veteran drew his sword. "Don't move," he told Kirk. "You'll only die harder."

As he lifted his weapon to strike, there was a wild cry. "*Murderers!*"

Flavius had raced into the arena, sword raised high. The startled Master of the Games wheeled to meet the onslaught. Guards were running to block the gladiator's rush; and Kirk, moving fast to help him, had almost reached him when every light in the place went out, plunging it into near darkness. Kirk hesitated for a split second. Then he used the dimness to fell a guard with a "space karate" blow. Another lunged for him. A smash with a sword butt sent him sprawling. There was a burst of submachine gunfire. Kirk, close to Flavius now, cried, "The cells! Which way?"

"The barred doors across . . ."

Flavius was cut down by another splatter of bullets. Kirk, realizing his danger, dodged a sword slash—and seizing the guard, spun him around to face the source of the gunfire. The man stumbled forward into the guard with the gun. He was thrown off balance—and Kirk, grabbing the gun, clubbed himself free. The lights came back as he reached the barred doors at the other side of the arena.

He was seen. Guards shouted. A submachine gun blast struck near him. He turned, firing a burst himself. It silenced the gunner. Kirk fired again at the heavy lock on the barred doors.

Their cell was at the middle of a corridor. "Look out!" Kirk yelled to them. His gun spit bullets at the cell's lock.

Spock kicked the door open and McCoy cried, "Jim! Are you all right?"

"What did they do to you, Captain?"

"They threw me—a few curves, Spock. Perhaps it's better if I don't talk about it now . . ."

He'd heard the sounds of pursuit. Guards had followed him, running. A javelin hurtled past them. Kirk aimed the gun. The men halted but one in the rear was raising the muzzle of his . . .

"Hold!"

It was Claudius. Guards ranged behind him; he stood at the other end of the corridor. In both directions escape was cut off.

"We're in each other's line of fire." Claudius spoke to the guards. "Swords only."

Both groups of guards, swords high, were moving in.

"But I can use my gun," Kirk said. "And in either direction, Claudius."

As he eyed the little Proconsul, he saw that Merik had joined him. Claudius moved away from him. "I pity you, 'Captain' Merik," he said. "But watch. At least *see* how men die."

A guard with a javelin raised his arm. Kirk whirled with the gun. It gave a click on an empty cylinder. The guards charged. Kirk downed the first with his gunstock.

Spock reached for his dropped sword and McCoy picked up the javelin beside him.

Merik came to a decision. Death was nearing the *Enterprise* men. They were fighting now back to back. Merik pulled the missing communicator from his pocket, clicking it open. "Starship, lock in on this place: three to . . ."

With a shocked look on his face, he staggered. Claudius withdrew the sword he'd driven into him. Merik glanced at his seducer; and choking on blood, whispered into the communicator, "Three to beam-up . . . emergency . . ."

As he fell, he threw the communicator to Kirk over the heads of the guards. The dead Bob Merrick of the Space Academy had finally made peace with himself. Already, before Claudius' astounded eyes, Kirk, Spock and McCoy were dematerializing into dazzle. Then even its sparkles were gone.

Kirk was dictating into his Captain's Log.

"Note commendation to Engineering Officer Scott for his performance in commanding this vessel during my absence. Despite enormous temptation and strong personal feelings, he obeyed the Prime Directive. His temporary 'blackout' of the city below resulted in no interference with its society and yet saved the lives of myself and the landing party. We are prepared to leave orbit shortly."

He punched his "off" button. Beside him, Scott, his face red with embarrassed pleasure, said, "Thank you, Captain. I'll see to the engines."

As he entered the bridge elevator, Spock and McCoy stepped out of it.

McCoy, approaching the command chair, said, "I just saw on your report that Flavius was killed. I'm sorry. I liked that huge sun-worshiper."

Spock spoke earnestly. "I wish we could have examined that belief of his more closely, Captain. It does seem illogical that sun-worshipers could evolve a philosophy of total brotherhood. Worship of the sun is almost always a primitive superstition-religion . . ."

Uhura had overheard. She turned from her console. "I'm afraid you have it wrong, Mr. Spock. All of you . . ."

Three pairs of eyes were on her. She went on. "I've

131

been monitoring old-style radio waves and heard talk about this brotherhood religion. Don't you understand? Not the sun in the sky . . . the *Son—the Son of God!*"

McCoy protested. "But when we mentioned stars, Septimus said they worshiped the sun up there."

But Kirk's face was thoughtful. "In most of our own religions, don't people tend to look upward when speaking of the Deity?" He paused. "Caesar and Christ . . . they *did* have both. And the word is spreading only now down there."

"A philosophy of total love, total brotherhood," McCoy said.

Spock nodded. "It will replace their Imperial Rome. And it will happen during their Twentieth century."

Remembering the arena's ferocity, Kirk said, "It would be something to watch, to be part of."

"How stupid of me not to have comprehended!" Spock exclaimed.

McCoy looked at him. "I tend to go along with that, Mr. Spock."

"Doctor . . . the next time I have an opportunity to save your life—"

"—you'll do the logical thing, save me." McCoy smiled. "Comforting to know that, Spock."

Something good had happened between the two, Kirk thought. He was glad. Both men were dear to him. It was high time they admitted how dear they were to each other. Though he knew how little their sparring meant, it was a waste of time that could be better spent. On the other hand, who knew? There were many ways of revealing affection.

He turned to Chekov. "Take us out of orbit, Mr. Chekov. Ahead, warp factor one."

"Aye, sir. Ahead, warp factor one."

Kirk looked at the viewing screen. The Earth-like planet that had confused itself with the Roman Empire was a diminishing pinpoint of light. Then it was gone.

Day of the Dove

(Jerome Bixby)

Though the planet had said it was under attack by an unidentified spacecraft, the *Enterprise* landing party had found only black dust, white rocks and strange clumps of moving plants. Its tricorders—McCoy's as well as Chekov's —refused to report any evidence of a colony or of people who could have signaled the message. Yet they had existed.

Kirk stooped for a handful of the black, powdery soil. "An SOS from a human settlement—one hundred men, women and children. All gone. Who did it? Why?"

As if in reply, his communicator beeped. "Spock here, sir. Sensors have picked up a Klingon ship closing in fast."

"Deflectors on, Mr. Spock! Protect yourselves. Total response if attacked." He closed the communicator, his face grim. So that was the answer—Klingons. They had destroyed the settlement. But Spock had more news of the Klingon ship. "Trouble aboard her, Captain. Evidence of explosions . . . massive damage. We never fired at her."

"Maintain full alert, Mr. Spock."

Behind his group the air was collecting into dazzle. Six Klingons in their stiff metallic tabards were materializing, their weapons aimed and ready. Their leader was the first to assume full shape. His hard, slant-eyed face distorted by fury, he reached out and swung Kirk around. "You attacked my ship!" he shouted. "Four hundred of my crew —dead! My vessel is disabled. I claim yours! You are prisoners of the Klingon Empire for committing a wanton act of war against it!" He nodded to his men. "Disarm them!"

Kirk had recognized the harsh, Mongol-like features. The Klingons' Kang. "We took no action against your ship," he said.

He'd been hustled into line with Chekov and McCoy. Kang paced before them. "For three years your Federation and our Empire have been at peace . . . a treaty we have honored to the letter . . ."

Kirk protested again. "We did not attack your ship."

"Were the screams of my men imaginary? What were your secret orders? To start a war? You have succeeded! Or maybe to test a new weapon. We shall be interested to examine it!"

Kirk said, "There was a Federation colony on this planet. *It* was destroyed."

"And by what? I see no bodies, no ruins. A colony of the invisible!"

"Perhaps a new *Klingon* weapon that leaves no traces. Federation ships don't specialize in sneak attacks!"

Along the ground near Kang a small, mushroom-shaped crystal was floating. Its swirling red color was concealed by a white rock and a faint, ugly throbbing came from it.

Kirk's patience was ebbing. No denial of guilt seemed able to penetrate the heavy bones of Kang's hairless skull. "You lured my ship into ambush with a false Klingon distress call!"

Kirk stared at him. "*You* received a distress call? *We* were the ones who received it!"

"I don't propose to spend any more time arguing your fantasies, Kirk! The *Enterprise* is ours! Instruct your Transporter Room. We are ready to beam aboard."

"Go to the devil," Kirk said.

"We have no devil—but we understand the habits of yours . . ." Still hidden among the rocks, the crystal's red glow brightened as Kang burst out, "I will torture you to death, one by one! Who will be the first? You, Kirk?"

Chekov suddenly exploded into action. He charged Kang, sobbing with rage. *"Swine! Filthy Klingon murderers!"* Kirk made a grab for him, missed—and Kang's men beat him to the ground. But he still sought to get at Kang. *"You killed my brother! Piotr!"*—the Arcanis Four Research Outpost . . . a hundred peaceful people massacred —*just as you did here! My brother, Piotr . . ."*

Kang looked down at him. "So you volunteer to join him. That is loyalty." He gestured to one of his men. A sputtering device was pushed against Chekov's neck. He writhed with agony, doubled up. Kirk, wrenching forward, was immobilized by the Klingons. The device was readjusted—and Chekov screamed.

"You win, Kang!" Kirk said. "Stop the torture!"

"Jim!" McCoy cried. "You can't hand over the *Enterprise!*"

"Help Chekov, Bones."

Kang was eyeing Kirk. "Don't plan any tricks. I will kill a hundred hostages at the first sign of treachery!"

"I'll beam you aboard the *Enterprise*. Once we're there—no tricks."

"Your word?"

Kirk nodded; and Chekov, still convulsed with pain, cried, "Captain!—we can't! . . . don't let these . . . *animals* . . . have the ship!"

"Animals?" Kang said. "Your captain crawls like one. A Klingon would not have surrendered." He turned to Kirk. "Order everyone in this area to be transported up." He said something to his men, and Kirk, ringed by weapons, opened his communicator.

"Kirk to *Enterprise*. Mr. Spock . . ."

"Here, Captain."

"We have guests," Kirk told him. "Adjust Transporter for wide-field and beam-up everyone in the target area." His finger pressed a tiny control on the communicator.

"Yes, Captain."

Everybody shimmered out, Kirk under the weapons, Chekov supported by McCoy, both glaring.

In the *Enterprise* Transporter Room, only the landing party materialized. No Klingons stood on the platform.

Kirk stepped off his pad. "Full Security on the double, Mr. Galloway! Good work, Spock!"

135

As Galloway hit the intercom, the bewildered McCoy said, "What—happened?"

"Landing party brought up intact," Spock told him.

At the console, Scott spoke. "All others suspended in transit. Who are the guests, by the way, Captain?"

"Klingons."

Scott grinned happily, slapping the console. "They're in here—until we decide to rematerialize them."

"Galloway?" Kirk said.

"Security squads on the way, sir."

Chekov's voice was thick with hate. "Captain! Leave them on the planet! Leave them where they are! In nonexistence. That's so many less Klingon monsters in the galaxy!"

"And that's what they would do." Kirk said. As the Security detail rushed through the door, he spoke to the Transporter Chief. "Bring them in."

The six Klingons sparkled into shape on the platform. They all stiffened, taking in the changed situation. Outnumbered by the Security men, they made no resistance as they were disarmed. The weaponless Kang looked at Kirk.

"Liar!" He spat the word.

"I said no tricks *after* we reached the ship." Kirk stepped forward, formal, terse. "You are prisoners of the United Federation of Planets against which you may or may not have committed an act of war."

"There are survivors still aboard my ship," Kang said.

Kirk nodded to the Transporter chief and Scott said, "Captain, we haven't been able to get through to Starfleet Command. All subspace frequencies are blocked. And there's too much radiation from the Klingon ship—it's a hazard to the vicinity."

"Prepare to destruct, Scotty."

"Completing the job you started!"

Kirk wheeled on Kang. "You wouldn't be standing there if I had."

The surviving Klingons were shimmering into form. Of the six, several were women. One, queenly, graceful, her dark eyes gleaming under the epicanthic fold of their Mongol lids, left the platform to go at once to Kang. He took her arm. "This is Mara—my wife and my Science officer," he told Kirk.

136

She ignored Kirk. "What has happened, Kang?"

"More Federation treachery. We are prisoners."

She was visibly terrified. The arm in Kang's hand trembled. "What will they do to us? I have heard of their atrocities . . . their death camps! They will torture us for our scientific and military information . . ."

Kirk addressed her. "You have some things to learn about us, madam." He turned to Galloway. "Detain them in the crew lounge. Program a food-synthesizer to accommodate our . . . guests. You will be well treated, Commander Kang."

"So I have seen," the Klingon said.

Kirk bowed and left, followed by Spock, McCoy and the still blazing Chekov. Unseen, unheard, the floating crystal hummed over their heads as they passed into the corridor.

"What *did* attack their ship, Jim?"

Kirk didn't answer. "Mr. Spock, maintain Red Alert. Scan this sector for other ships. Run a full check on the colony. We've got to nail this down fast . . ."

"We know what happened!" Chekov cried. "That distress call—"

Spock, speaking to nobody in particular, said, "From their distant position, the Klingons could scarcely have attacked the colony at the time we received the call. Moreover, they were apparently attracted there themselves by a distress call."

"Lies!" Chekov cried. "They want to start a war by pretending *we* attacked it!"

Entering an elevator, Kirk glanced at his overwrought face. But McCoy was saying, "Chekov may be right. The Klingons *claim* to have honored the truce—but there have been incidents! . . . raids on our outposts . . ."

"We've never proved the Klingons committed them, Bones."

McCoy was flushed with unusual vehemence. "What proof do we need? We know what a Klingon is!"

He stormed out of the elevator. Kirk frowned, puzzled by his belligerence; and Spock, noting his uneasiness, said, "Our Log-tapes will indicate our innocence in the present situation, Captain."

"Unfortunately, there is no guarantee they will be believed."

At the bridge deck, Chekov stalked to his post, his back stiff and stubbornly unrelenting. Kirk eyed him again before he asked for Uhura's report.

"Still unable to contact Starfleet Command, Captain. Outside communications blanketed."

"Keep at it, Lieutenant. We've got a diplomatic tiger by the tail."

He'd have liked authorization to take steps about the derelict Klingon ship. But at least he knew no lives were aboard it. He turned in his command chair. "Forward phasers locked and ready to fire, Mr. Sulu."

"Aye, sir."

"Fire phasers," Kirk said.

On the screen, the crippled vessel flared into light—and vanished. So that was that. A diplomatic tiger, indeed.

"Lieutenant Uhura?"

"No contact with Starfleet yet, sir."

Spock looked up from his mounded viewer. "Sensor sweeps reveal no other ships within range, Captain."

Had the Klingons annihilated that colony after all? There was no telling. Not now. He swung to Uhura. "Keep trying, Lieutenant. Mr. Sulu, set course seventeen mark four. Warp speed three."

"Warp three, sir."

In the crew lounge, Security guards and the "guests" were facing each other, each group wary, watchful, suspicious. Above them, all the crystal drifted. Kang, Mara beside him, used an empty space for restless pacing. "When I take this ship," he said, "I will have Kirk's head stuffed and hung on his cabin wall."

"They will kill us before we can act," she warned him.

"No! They wish to question us—learn our strength, our plans. They never will."

"We are forty," she protested. "Forty against four hundred."

One of Kang's men stepped forward. "Four thousand throats may be cut in one night by a running man."

"Patience," Kang said. "Vigilance. They will make

their mistake. Capture of the *Enterprise* will give us knowledge to end this war quickly."

The crystal's unheard throb moved out of the lounge and into the corridor. When it reached the bridge, its throbbing faded. Uhura, abruptly irritated, jabbed at her controls. "Still no outside contact, sir! Carriers normal. Channels open. I don't understand! Could the Klingons be doing something—?"

The ship suddenly shuddered. Engine sound rose. Kirk whirled. "Mr. Sulu?"

"Change of course, sir! Accelerating . . ." He struggled with switches. "Helm dead. Auxiliary navigation dead!"

Kirk braced himself against another shudder. "Override."

Sulu turned. "*Nothing* responds, Captain!"

"New course?"

"Nine-oh-two mark five . . ."

It would head the *Enterprise* out of the galaxy. Kirk hit a button. "Scotty—stop engines!"

The engine sound grew to a whining roar. On the intercom, Scott's voice was high with alarm. ". . . would if I could, sir! My controls have gone crazy! Something's— taken over . . ."

The bridge trembled under the rising roar. Scott shouted, "The engines, Captain! They've gone to warp nine—by themselves!"

Uhura's board was a dazzle of wildly flickering lights. Earphones fixed, she cried, "Captain! Reports from the lower decks! Emergency bulkheads closed! Almost four hundred crewmen trapped down there!"

Furious, Kirk exploded from his seat, racing for the elevator. The crystal followed him into the crew lounge. Kang was pleased with his information. "The bulk of your crew trapped? Your ship racing from the galaxy at wild speeds? Delightful! But how did I perform this sabotage, Kirk? My men are *here*."

Frigid with rage, Kirk spoke to Galloway. "Double security. Some Klingons may have beamed aboard, undetected. Mr. Spock, get down to Engineering. Help Scott hammer things back to normal and release those crewmen!"

139

He eyed Kang. "Before I throw you in the brig, I owe you something!" He landed a clenched fist on Kang's jaw. The Klingon stumbled back into a console, his hand falling on a lever. It came loose, grew red—and changed into a sword. Kang, amazed, stared at it in unbelief. Then he hefted it. At the same moment, all the lounge's objects—ashtrays, vases, lamps, magazines, game equipment—went into glow, transforming into swords, shields, javelins, battle-axes. The Klingons rushed for the weapons.

Kirk's people reached for their phasers. But the phasers, too, went into glow. Then they turned into swords and maces.

Kang took a swordsman's stance. "You killed four hundred of my men, Captain Kirk. It is time that that debt be repaid . . ."

Kirk looked at the sword that had been a console lever. Molecular revolution. But explanation did nothing to solve the deadly mystery. His own phaser was a sword.

The Klingons attacked—and the fight was on. Outnumbered, the Security guards were forced to retreat. Kirk fenced expertly, and was deflecting a slash by Kang when he saw that Galloway was wounded. He battled his way to the lieutenant, got an arm around him and shoved him into an elevator. The doors whooshed shut in the faces of Kang and his men. They rang with the sound of beating, frustrated swords.

Kirk beeped Engineering on his intercom. "The Klingons are free, Scotty. And armed. They'll try to take the ship. How many men do we have?"

"I don't know, sir, but three hundred and ninety-two are trapped below decks."

"Deploy forces to protect your section and Auxiliary Control Center. Check the Armory—and try to free those trapped men."

"Doors and bulkheads won't budge, sir. We'll have to cut through—"

"Blow out bulkheads if you have to—we need numbers! Any luck regaining control of speed?"

"No, sir. She's a projectile—at warp nine. Don't ask me what's holding her together."

"Five-minute reports. Kirk out."

He went to Spock's station. "Full sensor scans of the ship, Mr. Spock. Report any movements on the part of the Klingons. The Klingon Empire has maintained a dueling tradition. They think they can beat us with swords!"

Spock coolly examined the sword that had once been his phaser. "Neither the Klingon technology nor ours is capable of this, Captain. Instantaneous transmutation of matter. I doubt that they are responsible . . ."

"Other logical candidates?" Kirk demanded impatiently.

"None, Captain. But if they had such power, wouldn't they have created more effective weapons—and only for themselves?"

Kirk turned away. "Get below, Mr. Sulu. Take command of forces protecting Engineering and Auxiliary Control."

Sulu rose and Chekov rose with him.

"As you were, Mr. Chekov," Kirk said.

"*No*, sir! Let me go, too! I've got a personal score to settle with Klingons!"

"Maintain your post. This is no time for vendettas."

"Captain, I . . ."

"Sit down, Mister."

Chekov made a break for the elevator. As he reached it, Kirk grabbed his shoulder. Chekov wrenched away; and Spock, at Kirk's side, reached out an arm. Ducking under it, Chekov drew his sword. As he lifted it, Kirk and Spock paused, unwilling to risk a tangle that might hurt him.

"Don't try to stop me, Captain! I saw what they left of Piotr! I swore on his grave I would avenge his murder . . ." He backed into the elevator and its doors closed.

Sulu was staring. "What's Chekov's grudge against the Klingons? Who's—Piotr?"

"His brother," Kirk said. "Killed in a Klingon raid."

"His brother?" Sulu echoed blankly. "Chekov never had a brother! He's an only child."

It was Kirk's turn to stare. After a long moment, he said, "You are mistaken."

"I'm not, sir!" Sulu was very earnest. "I *know* he's an only child. It's why he requests his shore leaves on Earth —a good only son of his parents should visit them!"

"On your way to Engineering, Mr. Sulu."

Sulu left—and a newly troubled Kirk hit his intercom. "Captain Kirk to Security. Find Mr. Chekov and return him to the bridge."

Uhura swung around. "Captain—what could have made Chekov believe he had a brother?"

"I don't know, Lieutenant. But he does believe it—and now he wants revenge for a nonexistent loss."

On the *Enterprise* bridge, mystery was compounding itself, but in its crew lounge, clarification was in order.

A Klingon had projected the Starship's plan and arrangements on the viewer. "Layout and specifications of the ship, Commander Kang."

"Enemy numbers are the same as ours," Mara said. "We have a fighting balance."

"Then we will take this ship!" Kang spoke with a ferocious determination.

"A vessel that is racing toward the edge of the galaxy is weakening," his man said. "If the humans can't control it . . ."

Kang jabbed at the diagrams on the viewer. "These points we must capture! First, their Engineering section . . ."

McCoy was working feverishly to complete his treatment of Galloway's wound. As he worked, he could hear the moans of other slashed men waiting their turn at the table.

"Those—filthy butchers!" he muttered. "There are *rules*—even in *war* . . . you don't keep on hacking at a man after he's down!" He felt sick with impotent rage. He looked at an orderly who was wiping blood from a shoulder gash. "Where's that Numanol capsule?"

Haggard and worn by Sickbay's harrowing activity, the orderly turned, only to be confronted by wheeled stretchers bearing two more injured men. McCoy went to them. A glance told him their wounds were serious. As he bent over one of them, he spoke to the orderly. "I'm convinced now the only good Klingon is a dead one," he said.

Scott was inclined to agree with him. All attempts to release the cut-off crewmen had failed. Phaser beams couldn't cut through the bulkheads. Their metal's structure had changed. He hit an intercom button to make his report.

"What about the Armory?" Kirk said.

"I'm there now, Captain. You never saw such a collection of antiques in your life . . ."

The Armory had turned into a medieval weapons' Wonderland. Crossbows, hatchets, knives, broadswords . . .

"Get back to Engineering," Kirk said. "Keep trying to reestablish engine control. And make some phasers—fast."

"Aye, sir."

He was about to leave when he spotted a sharply two-edged weapon in the rack. He removed it, fondling it. "A claymore!" Exchanging it for the sword at his waist, he murmured, "Ah, you're a beauty, aren't you?"

As he strutted out of the Armory, reinforced by Scotland's history of claymore triumphs, Spock was computing the opposing forces at an exact thirty-eight. He lifted his head from his computer. "The Klingons occupy Deck Six and starboard Deck Seven, Captain. We control all sections above." He bent to his viewer again, becoming suddenly intent. "Most curious," he said.

"What?" Kirk said.

"There appear to be more energy units aboard than can be accounted for by the presence of the *Enterprise* crew plus the Klingons. A considerable discrepancy."

"Could some more of Kang's crew have beamed aboard?"

"Their ship was thoroughly vacated, Captain." He flipped a switch. "I shall compensate for the human and Klingon readings."

The crystal had found Engineering. It hovered high in the air, as unseen as it was unheard.

Scotty, descending a ladder, stepped down into the lower level of his section. "Any signs of those treacherous devils, Mr. Sulu?"

"All clear, Mr. Scott."

Klingons, moving into the upper level, leaped down to the attack. The surprised humans fell back. But Scott was inspired by his claymore's tradition. He felled a Klingon with its haft; and then realizing that his species was hopelessly outnumbered, darted through a door into the corridor. Sulu joined him, downing the two Klingons who followed him.

Scott was breathless. "I don't know how many of these creatures are around. We'll split up here. Maybe . . . one of us . . . can make it back to the bridge."

Inside Engineering, the rest of the crew were being shoved against a wall. As they were disarmed, a jubilant Kang strode in, Mara at his side.

It was hard going, trying to get back to the bridge. Klingons seemed to be everywhere. The canny Scott finally reconciled national glory with common sense. He hid in a lavatory. So he was in no position to see Spock zero in on an unusual but steady beeping.

"An alien life force, Captain. A single entity. I am unable to ascertain its location." He flicked a switch. "Readings diverted to the library computer for analysis . . ."

Kirk, beside him, said, "We have to make contact . . . find out what it wants!"

Calmer than custard, Spock said, "The computer report, Captain . . ."

There was a click—and the computer voice said, "Alien life force on board is composed of pure energy. Type unknown. Actions indicate intelligence and purpose."

"What purpose?" Spock said.

The metallic computer voice said, "Insufficient data for further analysis."

The computer's stark admission of inadequacy fired Kirk into new, creative thought. Out of his human memory banks he made connections. "A brother that never existed," he said. "A phantom colony—fancied distress calls! The illusion that phasers are swords! Do you begin to sense a pattern, Mr. Spock?"

Spock, loyal to facts, looked up. "If the alien has caused these phenomena, it is apparently able to manipulate matter and minds."

"Now it's controlling the *Enterprise*—taking us out of the galaxy! *Why?*"

"I am constrained to point out, Captain, that as minds are evidently being influenced, we cannot know that our own memories at this moment are accurate."

Kirk faced his sole alternative. "We've got to talk to Kang and bury the hatchet!"

"An appropriate choice of terms, sir. However, once blood has been drawn, it is notoriously difficult to arrange a truce with Klingons . . ."

"A *truce?*"

It was McCoy—an outraged, infuriated McCoy. His white surgical uniform was blood-spattered. "I've got seven men down in Sickbay—some of them dying—*atrocities* committed on their persons! And you can talk of making peace with those fiends? They'd jump us the minute our backs were turned! We know what Klingons do to prisoners! Slave labor, death planets—experiments!"

Kirk had never seen Bones so angry. "McCoy—" he began.

McCoy rushed on. "Even while you're talking, the Klingons are planning attacks! This is a fight to the death —and we'd better start trying to win it!"

"We are trying to end it, Doctor." Spock's voice was more than usually quiet. "There is an alien aboard which may have created this situation . . ."

McCoy glared at him. "Who *cares* what started it! We're *in* it! Those murderers! Let's wipe out every one of them!"

"Bones, the alien is the enemy we have to wipe out—"

Uhura cut in. "Sickbay calling, Doctor. There are more wounded men requiring your attention."

McCoy wheeled, starting back to the elevator. Then he turned again to Kirk and Spock. "How many men have to die before you begin acting like military men instead of damn fools?" The elevator doors closed on his bleakly hopeless face. Kirk looked at Spock. The Vulcan murmured, "Extraordinary."

Kang was on the intercom. Kirk spoke quickly. "There's something important we must discuss . . ."

Vindictive and triumphant, Kang's voice said, "I have captured your Engineering section! I now control this ship's power and life support systems." At Engineering's intercom he nodded to Mara. She moved a series of switches and Kang spoke again into the intercom.

"I have deprived all areas of life support except our

145

own. You will die . . . of suffocation . . . in the icy cold of space . . ."

On the bridge, lights were dimming. Panels were going dark.

Kirk walked slowly over to Sulu's station. "Mr. Sulu, get down to Emergency Manual Control. Try to protect life support circuits and activate auxiliary power . . ."

"Aye, Captain." But as Sulu approached the elevator, Scott burst out of it. He barely acknowledged the helmsman's smile of relief at his safety. Kirk went to him. "Scotty! I'm glad you escaped . . ."

Scott was shaking. "Chekov was right, Captain! We *should've* left those slant-eyed goons in the Transporter! That's right where they belong—in nonexistence! Now they can study the *Enterprise*—add our technology to theirs—change the balance of power!" He lurched at Kirk, not in attack but in a blind misery that was seeking some shred of comfort. "You've jeopardized the Federation!"

The charge was a cry of anguish. "Scotty . . ."

Spock had joined them. "Mr. Scott, calm yourself," he said.

Scott pulled back. For one terrible moment, Kirk feared he was going to spit at Spock, such aversion showed in his face. "Keep your Vulcan hands off me! Just stay away! Your 'feelings' might get hurt, you green-blooded, halfbreed freak!"

Kirk didn't believe his ears. Appalled, he stared at Scott. Then Spock made his icy retort. "Let me say that I have not enjoyed serving with humans. I find their illogical and foolish emotions a constant irritant."

"So transfer out!" Scott shouted.

Spock moved toward Scott. He loomed darkly formidable over him—and Scott, frightened, took a clumsy punch at him. Kirk grabbed their arms; but Spock, twisting easily free, seemed about to use his great strength in an upsurge of rage he couldn't govern. Kirk tried again; and yanking them apart, crashed back into his command chair. "Spock! Scotty! Stow it!" He pinned them, panting. *"What's happening to us! What are we saying to each other?"*

Spock pushed Kirk away. Kirk braced himself, ready for some ultimate disaster. But nothing happened. Spock

146

was himself again, perhaps a little more impassive than usual.

"Fascinating," he said to Kirk. "A result of stress, Captain?"

"We've been under stress before! It hasn't set us at each other's throats!" Scott had started forward again and Kirk pushed him back.

"This is a *war*!" Scott yelled.

"There isn't any war . . ." Kirk paused, the sound of his own words in his ears. "Or—*is* there?"

"Have we forgotten how to defend ourselves?" Scott cried.

"Shut up, Scotty." Kirk paced at the back of his command chair, frowning as he put his two's together. "What *is* happening to us? We're trained to think in other terms—than war! We're trained to fight its causes whenever possible! So why are *we* reacting like savages?" The two's were adding up. He swung around to his men. "There are two forces on this ship, armed equally. Has—a war been *staged* for us? A war complete with weapons, grievances, patriotic drumbeats?" He turned on Scott. "Even race hatred!"

Spock had nodded. "Recent events *would* seem directed to a magnification of basic human and Klingon hostilities. Apparently, it is by design that we fight. We seem to be pawns."

"In what game?" Kirk said. "Whose game? What are the rules?"

"It is most urgent," Spock said, "that we locate the alien entity, determine its motives—and some means of halting its activities."

Scott's startled thoughts had been tumbling around in his head. He was quieter now—and guilt-stricken. He spoke to Spock. "Without sensors, sir? All our power down? The thing can pass through walls. It could be anywhere."

Kirk hit his intercom. "Mr. Sulu, report!"

Sulu was at the Jeffries tube, peering up into it. "No good, Captain. Circuits are in but systems aren't responding." As he spoke, the tube's complex instruments flickered with light and settled down to a steady pattern. He heard Kirk say, "Are we getting something?"

147

"Aye, sir. Power and life support restored—remotes on standby . . ."

"Good work!" Kirk told him.

"But Captain—*I didn't do it!* Everything just came on by itself!"

Kirk thought, "Well, this is a gift horse I don't look too close in the mouth of." He said, "All right, Mr. Sulu. Get back to Manual Control. Kirk out."

The bridge lights had come back to normal. Panels had resumed their humming. Spock turned. "Sensors operating again, Captain."

"Start scanning, Mr. Spock. Look for the alien."

In Engineering, a puzzled Mara was studying lights on a large board. "Their life support systems have resumed and are holding steady," she told Kang.

"Cause them to be unsteady," he said.

"They appear to be controlled from another location." For the first time her voice was uncertain. "I'm also unable to affect the ship's course—to return to our Empire."

"Some trick of Kirk's? Has he bypassed these circuits? What power is it that supports our battle, yet starves our victory? Interrupt power at their main life support couplings. Where are they?"

She looked at the diagrams on the viewer. "They are on this deck." At Kang's nod, she spoke to a Klingon. "Come with me."

Above them in the bridge, Spock had tensed. He whirled to Kirk. "Alien detected, Captain! In the Engineering level, near reactor number three!"

Kirk leaped from his chair. "Let's go!"

Mara, the Klingon behind her, was rushing down a corridor that led to the couplings. As they passed an alcove, Chekov, sword drawn, moved out of it, his face hate-filled. Two well-aimed slashes disposed of the Klingon. Mara was turning to run when Chekov grabbed her and whirled her around. She fought well; but Chekov blocked her karate blow. He pinned her back against the wall, sword at her throat. It was a lovely throat. Chekov's manner changed. He eyed her with an ugly speculation, grinning. "No, you don't die—yet," he said. "You're not human but you're beautiful, aren't you?" His grip on her tightened. "Just how human *are* you?"

She pushed at him, struggling against the grip. Chekov placed his hand over her mouth and was pressing her into the alcove when Kirk and Spock raced out of the elevator. Assault was the last thing on their minds. Hearing Mara's muffled scream, they stared at each other. Then they broke into a run, rounded a corner—and stopped dead in their tracks at what they saw.

"Chekov!"

Chekov wheeled to face Kirk, a wild beast deprived of its prey. Mara's garment was ripped from her shoulders. Chekov spun her away. She hit a wall and dropped. He tried to dodge Kirk and failed. Kirk seized him, slapping his face forehand, backhand. Chekov sobbed; and raising his sword, made a swipe at Kirk. He was disarmed and felled with a punch. Beside himself with fury, Kirk struck him again.

Spock put a hand on Kirk's shoulder. "Captain . . . he is not responsible . . ."

Mara, crouched on the deck, was trying to pull her torn clothes together. Kirk went to her. "Listen to me," he said. "There's an alien entity aboard this ship. It's forcing us to fight. We don't know its motives—we're trying to find out. Will you help us? Will you take me to Kang . . . a temporary truce! That's all I ask!"

Mingled fear and hate blazed from her eyes. Kirk turned his back on her. "Bring her, Spock." He moved to the weeping Chekov and lifted him gently in his arms. Was this what was in store for all of them? Hatred, violence wherever they turned?

McCoy was re-dressing Galloway's wound when Kirk carried Chekov into Sickbay. He looked up, taking them all in, Kirk, the still sobbing Chekov clinging to him, a disheveled Mara, closely followed by Spock. Shaking his head, he left Galloway and hurried to help Kirk place Chekov on an exam table. He applied a device to the new patient's head.

"Brainwaves show almost paranoid mania. What happened, Jim?"

"He's—lost control—useless as a fighter." He turned to the door. "Come on, Spock . . ."

McCoy stopped him with a hand on his arm. He seemed somewhat calmer himself but his tired face was be-

149

wildered. "*Jim*—Galloway's heart wound has almost entirely healed! The same with the other casualties. Sword wounds . . . into vital organs—massive trauma, shock—and they're all healing at a fantastic rate!"

Spock spoke. "The entity would appear to want us alive."

". . . Why?" Kirk said. "So we can fight and fight—and always come back for more? Some kind of bloody Colosseum? What next? The roar of crowds?"

Galloway was listening. And he was buying none of it. His jaw hardened. He wanted out from Sickbay and for only one reason—another crack at the Klingons.

Kirk felt the lieutenant's hostility like a tangible thing. "Spock, let's find that alien!" He looked at Mara. "You come along. Maybe we can prove to you that it exists!"

In the corridor, Spock unlimbered his tricorder. He led the way, searching cautiously, the tricorder first aimed one way, then another. When they reached a second intersection, Spock paused, gesturing to his left. They turned the corner—and they all heard the crystal's faint humming. Without speaking, Spock signaled them to look up to the right side of the corridor. The crystal was floating there, brighter than it had ever been.

Kirk shot a significant look at Mara. Now that she was forced to believe, she was staring at the thing's swirling red.

"What is it?" Kirk said.

"Totally unfamiliar, Captain."

Kirk approached the crystal. "What do you want? Why are you doing all this?" It hovered silently, persistent.

Kirk, close to blowing his stack, shouted, *"What do you want?"*

The thing glowed still brighter, bobbing slightly. Spock, noting the increased glow, whirled at a sound. Galloway, still bandaged, was coming down the corridor, a little weak but grimly determined. He hefted his sword—and started to push past them as though he didn't see them.

"Lieutenant Galloway!" Kirk cried. "What are you doing here? Did the Doctor release you?"

"I'm releasing myself!"

First, Chekov's insubordination. Now this one. It took

150

all Kirk's strength to remember that the crystal was in the business of war, dissension and rule-breaking.

"Go back to Sickbay," he said.

"Not on your life! I'm fit and ready for action!" He shook Kirk's hand from his arm. "The Klingons nearly put me away for good! I'm going to get me some scalps . . ."

"I order you!" Kirk said.

"I've got my orders! I'm obeying orders! To Kill Klingons! It's them or us, isn't it?"

The crystal had bobbed over Galloway's head. Spock, looking up, saw it bob as Galloway pushed past him, heading for an elevator. He tagged the man with a neck pinch. Kirk saw Galloway slump, unconscious, to the deck. Spock's eyes were already back on the crystal. Its glow had faded.

"Most interesting," Spock said.

His eyes returned to Kirk. "During Mr. Galloway's emotional outburst—his expressions of hatred and lust for vengeance—the alien's life-energy level *increased*. When the lieutenant became unconscious, the alien *lost* energy."

"A being that subsists on the emotions of others?" Kirk said.

"Such creatures are not unknown, Captain. I refer you to the Drella of Alpha Carinae five—energy creatures who are nourished by the cooperation of love they feel for one another." He had neared the crystal and was looking up at it, composed and calm. "This creature appears to be strengthened by mental radiations of hostility, by violent intentions . . ."

"It feeds—on hate!" Complete illumination dawned on Kirk.

"Yes, to put it simply, Captain. And it has acted as a catalyst to create this situation in order to satisfy that need. It has drawn fighting forces together, supplied crude weapons to promote the most violent mode of conflict. It has spurred racial animosities—"

"And kept numbers and resources balanced to maintain a stable state of violence! Spock, it's got to have a vulnerable area. It's got to be stopped!"

"Then all hostile attitudes on board must be eliminated, sir. The fighting must end—and soon."

151

Kirk nodded. "I agree. Otherwise, we'll be a doom ship—traveling forever between galaxies . . . filled with bloodlust . . . eternal warfare! Kang *has* to listen—we've got to pool our knowledge to get rid of that thing!"

The crystal was showing agitation, bobbing as though angry that its secret was known. Now, as Kirk strode to an intercom, it moved toward him, throbbing loudly. For a moment Kirk wavered. Then he walked on. The crystal, its hum furious, approached Mara. Suddenly, without warning, she hurled herself at Kirk, biting, scratching, pushing him away from the intercom. Spock lifted her from Kirk, quietly pinning her arms to her sides.

Kirk hit all buttons. "Kang! This is Kirk! Kang! *Kang!*"

Mara shrieked, "Commander! It's a trick! They are located—"

Spock's steel hand went over her mouth. At the intercom, Kirk hit the buttons again. *"Kang!"* It was hopeless. The Klingon wouldn't answer.

"The alien is affecting his mind, Captain. Soon it will grow so powerful that none of us will be able to resist it."

The intercom beeped and Kirk hit it fast—fast and hopefully. "Kirk here!"

"Scotty, sir. The ship's dilithium crystals are deteriorating. We can't stop the process . . ."

Kirk struck the wall with his fist. "Time factor, Scotty?"

"In twelve minutes we'll be totally without engine power, sir."

"Do everything you can. Kirk out."

The crystal stopped bobbing. It glowed brilliantly, back in the driver's seat. As they watched it, it vanished through a wall. Kirk spoke to Mara. "So we drift forever . . . with only hatred and bloodshed aboard. Now do you believe?"

Her strained eyes stared into his. But she made no answer.

The dilithium crystals were still losing power. Spock, rallying all his scientific know-how, toured the bridge, examining panels. Finally, he broke the bad news to Kirk. There was nothing to be done to halt the crystals' decay.

"We have nine minutes and fifty-seven seconds before

power zero," he said. "But there is a logical alternative, Captain." He was looking at Mara, his face speculative. "Kang's wife, after all, is our prisoner. A threat made to him . . ."

"*That's* something the Klingons would understand," Scott urged.

Mara had flinched, remembering the unspeakable atrocities said to be visited on Klingon prisoners by their human captors. Kirk saw her remembering them. Though the idea of using her to threaten Kang just might result in a productive discussion with him, it revolted him. On the other hand, peace between them was the sole hope now. After a long, painful moment, he said, "You're right, Mr. Spock."

He flicked on his intercom. This was going to be difficult. He harshened his voice. "Kang. Kang! This is Captain Kirk. I know you can hear me . . . Don't cut me off! *We have Mara—your wife!*"

At Engineering's intercom, Kang was listening. Kirk's voice went on. "We talk truce *now*—or she dies. Reply!"

Kang was silent.

"She has five seconds to live, Kang! Reply!"

The answer came. "She is a victim of war, Captain. She understands." Kang flicked off the intercom, his dark emotion visible to his men. He turned to them. "When we get Kirk, he is mine," he said.

The last card had been played. Kirk looked at Mara. She had stiffened, her head held high, proud, a queen awaiting death. He pointed to a seat. "Sit over there and keep out of our way. Lieutenant Uhura, guard her."

She didn't understand. ". . . you're . . . not going to . . . ?"

"The Federation doesn't kill or mistreat its prisoners. You've heard fables, propaganda." He looked away from her as though he'd forgotten her existence. "How much time now, Mr. Spock?"

"Eight minutes and forty-two seconds, sir."

Instead of taking a seat, Mara had gone to the panel Spock was studying. Reading it, she realized the dilithium situation. Near her, Uhura watched her as she turned in shocked belief. "So it was no trick . . ." she said, bewildered.

Scott spoke. "The alien has done all this. We are in its power. Our people—and yours."

Kirk rose from his chair. "We wanted only to end the fighting to save us all," he told her.

Her relief had bred a need to explain. "We have always fought, Captain Kirk. We must. We are hunters, tracking and taking what we need. There are poor planets in the Klingon systems. We must push outward to survive."

"Another way to survive is mutual trust, Mara. Mutual trust and mutual help."

"I will help you now," she said.

He'd hoped to no point too many times to feel anything but skepticism. "How?" he said.

"I will take you to Kang. I will add my plea to yours."

Scott's suspicion found voice. "Captain—I wouldn't trust her . . ."

"We can't get past the Klingon defenses in time now, anyway—" Kirk paused. "Unless . . ." He whirled to Spock. *"Spock! Intra*ship beaming! From one part of the ship to another! Is it possible?"

"It has rarely been done, sir, because of the great danger involved. Pinpoint accuracy is needed. If the Transportee should materialize within any solid object—a wall or deck . . ."

"Prepare the Transporter," Kirk said.

"Mr. Scott, please help me with the Main Transporter Board." Spock moved to a panel but Scott hesitated, worried.

"Even if it works, Captain, she may be leading you into a trap!"

"We're all in a trap, Scotty. And this is our only way out of it."

"We'll go with you, sir . . ."

"That would start the final battle." Kirk took a long-searching look at Mara. "I believe her."

Scott took one for himself. He believed her, too. "Aye, sir," he said.

Mara entered the elevator. Following her, Kirk said, "We'll wait for your signal." As the doors closed, Scott thoughtfully fingered his sword. "But she can't guarantee that Kang will listen. Right, Mr. Spock?"

But Spock was intent on the Main Transporter Board. "No one can guarantee another's actions, Mr. Scott."

The Transporter Room was empty. Entering it, Kirk deliberately removed his sword; and, disarmed, placed the weapon on the console. Mara smiled at him. Spock's voice spoke from the intercom. "Your automatic setting is laid in, Captain. When the Transporter is energized, you will have eight seconds to get to the pads."

The console was flickering with lights. As Kirk pressed a button, it beeped to every second that passed. Its hum rose and Kirk said, "I hope your computations are correct, Mr. Spock."

"You will know in five point two seconds, Captain."

Kirk and Mara went quickly into position on the platform. There were eight more beeps from the console before they shimmered out.

At their appearance in Engineering, the startled Kang exploded to his feet. *"Mara!* You are alive! . . . and you bring us a prize!" He turned, shouting, *"Guards!"*

Swords drawn, his men ringed Kirk.

"Kang—wait!" Mara cried. "He has come alone—unarmed! *He must talk to you!"*

"Brave Captain. What about?" Kang swung to his men. "Kill him."

Mara rushed into place before Kirk. *"No!* You must listen! There is great danger to us all!"

Kang paused—and Kirk moved her aside, unwilling to allow her shield to him. "Before you start killing," he said, "give me one minute to speak!"

Kang ignored him. He spoke to Mara. "What have they done to you? How have they affected your mind?" Then he spotted her torn garment, her bruised shoulder. His slanted eyes went icy. "Ah, I see why this human beast did not kill you . . ."

She flashed into action. She seized a sword and tossed it to Kirk. He caught it as Kang launched himself headlong into attack. Defending himself, he retreated before another fierce slash. Mara, held by a Klingon, was struggling, agonized by the turn events had taken.

"They didn't harm me! Kang, listen to Kirk!"

Kang backed away for another onrush. "With his death, we win!"

155

"Nobody wins!" Kirk shouted. "Have any of your men died?" He broke into sudden attack but only to bring himself closer to Kang. *"Listen! We can't be killed—any of us! "There's an alien aboard this ship that needs us alive!"*

Kang shoved him away only to come back with another vicious onslaught.

"You *fool!*" Mara screamed.

From behind them all, the Transporter humming sounded. Spock, McCoy, Sulu and the *Enterprise* forces sparkled into shape and substance. Kang's men rushed forward, swords aimed. The Security guards, led by Sulu who uttered a yell that might have been "Banzai!" closed with them.

Kirk, downing a Klingon with a hard right to the jaw, reached Kang—and grabbed him. Nose to nose, he shouted, *"Listen* to me! Let me *prove* what I say!"

Kang wrenched free, his sword up for the lethal downsweep. Kirk parried the blow in mid-descent. Mara, huddled against a wall, covered her face with her hands, despairing. Kang came back with another vicious slash. As Kirk ducked it, he heard the triumphant throbbing. He looked up. The crystal—above their heads, brighter than he'd ever seen it—was casting its virulent red light on Kang's face.

The sight was all that he needed. He pushed Kang back, pinning him, and whirled him around to face their common enemy.

"LOOK! *Up there!"*

Kang looked. He shot a glance at Kirk—but the real meaning of what he'd seen didn't get through to him.

The fight went on, interminably. Sulu plunged his sword into an opponent's chest. The Klingon staggered, pawing at the wound. Then he rallied. He drove so straight for Sulu's heart that the *Enterprise* helmsman barely managed to escape the thrust.

Kang, his eyes on the crystal, was just beginning to get the lay of the land. Kirk pressed his advantage. ". . . for the rest of our lives, Kang! For a thousand lifetimes— fighting, this insane violence! That alien over our heads will control us forever!"

The crystal throbbed loudly. Kirk himself felt the heat

of its bloody radiance. But Kang still twisted, snarling, avid for killing. Kirk smashed the sword that had reappeared in his hand. He struck it furiously against a bulkhead. It broke. Kang stared at him. Then he stepped forward, his own weapon upraised. Kirk stood his ground.

"Come on! In the brain, the heart—it doesn't matter, Kang! *I won't stay dead!* Next time the thing will see to it that I kill you. And you won't stay dead! The good old game of war—mindless pawn against mindless pawn! While something somewhere sits back and laughs . . . laughs fit to kill, Kang—and starts it all over again . . ."

The sword was at his throat.

"Jim—*jump him!*" McCoy shouted.

Spock spoke out of his wise Vulcan heritage. "Those who hate and fight must stop themselves, Doctor—or it is not stopped."

Mara had flung herself at Kang's feet. "I'm your wife —a Klingon! Would I lie for them? Listen to Kirk. He is telling the truth!"

"*Then be a pawn!*" Kirk said. "A toy—the good soldier who never asks questions!"

Kang looked up at the excitedly throbbing crystal. Very slowly, his hand relaxed on the sword. It dropped to the deck.

"Klingons," he told the crystal, "kill for their *own* purposes." He turned to his men, shouting. "Cease hostilities! At rest!"

They were puzzled by the order—but they obeyed. Kang yanked a Klingon away from a downed Security man. "*At rest! At rest!* You heard the order!"

Through the open door they could all hear the clashing sounds of continuing battle in other parts of the ship. "*All* fighting must be stopped, Captain, if the alien is to be weakened before our fuel is gone."

Kang had lifted Mara to her feet. They joined Kirk at the intercom as he activated it, Kang still suspicious.

"Lieutenant Uhura, put me on shipwide intercom . . ."

"Ready, Captain."

"Attention, all hands! A truce is ordered . . . the fighting is over! Regroup and lay down weapons." He stepped back, speaking urgently. "Kang! Your turn at the intercom . . ."

The Klingon hesitated, reluctant. He couldn't resist a push at Kirk as he moved to the intercom. "This is Kang. Cease hostilities. Disarm."

The crystal was bobbing wildly with anger; but its throbbing had lessened and its redness was dimmer. "The cessation of violence appears to have weakened the alien," Spock said. "I suggest that good spirits might prove to be an effective weapon."

Kirk nodded. A hard smile on his lips, he addressed the crystal. "Get off my ship!" The thing retreated, still bobbing. "You're powerless here. You're a dead duck. We know all about you—and we don't want to play your game any more."

The throbbing was fainter. Spock was right. What the invader needed was a cheerful scorn. Kirk looked up at it. "Maybe there are others like you still around. Maybe you've caused a lot of suffering—a lot of history. That's all over. We'll be on guard . . . we'll be ready for you. Now butt out!" He laughed at the crystal. "Haul it!"

McCoy waved a contemptuous hand. "Get out, already!" he yelled.

As the throbbing faded, Kirk was amazed to hear a hoarse chuckle from Kang. Then he laughed as though he weren't used to it. His gusto grew. "Out!" he shouted at the crystal. "We need no urging to hate humans!" He laughed harder at Spock's irritated glance. "But for the present—only fools fight in a burning house."

Guffawing, he rattled Kirk's teeth with a sadistic whack on the back. McCoy nudged Spock. After a moment, the Vulcan thumbed his nose at the crystal. "You will please leave," he said.

The red was now a dull flicker. They all watched it, laughing. Suddenly the crystal vanished through a bulkhead. Floating in space outside the Starship, it flared up and winked out.

The forced laughter had come hard. Kirk's relief from hours of nervous strain overwhelmed him so that he wasn't surprised to see that swords and shields had disappeared. Spock and McCoy discovered their phasers in place. McCoy made a point of drawing his; and Kang, noting the weapon, went right on chuckling. Caution—it was how things were between the Federation and his Klingon Empire.

Uhura's voice spoke. "Captain, jettisoning of fuel has stopped. The trapped crewmen are free. All systems returning to normal."

"Carry on, Lieutenant. Mr. Sulu, resume your post. Set course for—well, set it for any old star in the galaxy!"

As Sulu left, Kirk nearly knocked Kang from his feet with a mighty thump on the back. Kang spun around, blood in his eye—and Kirk grinned at him. *"Friends!"* he said.

The command chair was a place again where a man could relax. For a moment, anyway. Kirk leaned back in his seat.

"Ahead, Mr. Sulu. Warp one." He turned to Kang and Mara. "We'll reach a neutral planet by tomorrow. You'll be dropped there. No war, this time."

He eyed Mara. A real woman, that one. If she hadn't been Kang's wife . . . if there had been time. Ah well, no man could accommodate all opportunities . . .

Kang was saying, "Why do you humans revere peace? It is the weakling's way. There's a galaxy to be taken, Kirk, with all its riches!"

Spock looked up. "Two animals may fight over a bone, sir—or they can pool their abilities, hunt together more efficiently and share justly. Curiously, it works out about the same."

Kang turned. "One animal must trust the other animal."

"Agreed," Kirk said. "Cooperate . . . or fight uselessly throughout eternity. A universal rule you Klingons had better learn." He paused. *"We did."*

Had it got through? Maybe. At any rate, Kang's face seemed unusually thoughtful.

Plato's Stepchildren

(Meyer Dolinsky)

The planet was uncharted; but the sensors of the *Enterprise,* in orbit around it, had detected mineral and chemical riches under its rugged, mountainous surface. Spock looked up from his viewer to say briefly, "Kironide deposits, too, Captain."

"Record coordinates," Kirk told him.

Uhura turned. "Mr. Spock, what *is* kironide?"

"A particularly potent and long-lasting source of power, Lieutenant—very rare."

She was about to question him further when her board's lights flashed. Surprise still on her face, she reported to Kirk. "A distress signal's coming in, Captain."

It *was* disconcerting news. An uncharted planet, apparently uninhabited—and an SOS call. Kirk said, "Let's have it. Put it on audio, Lieutenant."

A woman's voice, amplified by the bridge's audio system, was loud enough for everyone to hear.

"My spouse is dying. We need a physician immediately. The situation is urgent. If there's a physician hearing this, we need you. Please make contact. My spouse is dying . . ."

Kirk said, "I thought there was no life down there, Mr. Spock."

"The sensors still read negative, sir."

But the voice was still with them. "Please help us. We are in desperate need of a physician. My spouse is dying. Acknowledge . . . acknowledge . . . please . . ."

"Mr. Spock, life forms or no life forms, that distress call sounds authentic." Kirk got up and strode to Uhura's station. "Lieutenant, acknowledge and report that we're beaming down at once. Notify Dr. McCoy to meet us in the Transporter Room."

Medikit in hand, McCoy materialized with Kirk and Spock in front of a colonnaded promenade. At first glance, there seemed to be no one around. Then Kirk spotted movement at the rear of a marble column. A dwarf, clearly frightened and wearing a short Greek robe that left one misshapen shoulder bare, broke from behind the column and scuttled to them.

"Are you from the spaceship *Enterprise?*"

Kirk looked down at him for a moment before he spoke. "That's right."

"No offense," the dwarf said hastily. He bowed low. "Alexander . . . at your service. I sing, I dance, I play all variety of games and I'm a good loser. A very good loser. And I try, I try very hard. Please bear that in mind."

It was an extraordinary speech. The *Enterprise* men looked at each other, nonplussed, and the dwarf said, "Now, if you'll accompany me . . ."

"Who inhabits this planet?" Kirk said.

The little creature bowed again. "Platonians. You've never heard of us. Our home star is Sahndara. Millennia ago, just before it novaed, we got off. Our leader liked Plato's ideas—Plato—Platonians, see? In fact, Parmen, our present philosopher-king, calls us Plato's children. Some of us think we're more like *step*children." He gave a nervous little laugh. "Now, please—they're waiting for you . . ."

He wheeled around and hurried ahead of them like a mechanical doll set suddenly into motion.

The *Enterprise* three hesitated. Then, curious but a little uneasy, they followed him.

Whoever McCoy's prospective patient was, he had done very well for himself. The dwarf ushered them into a stately, atrium-like court pillared by marble. In the center of the place, a nymph of marble dripped water from an urn into a reflecting pool. There was a game board on the left, flanked by benches, the pieces it held geometrically shaped into balls, pyramids, cylinders and cubes. Two tall robed men stood near a couch where another one reclined, his legs covered. Kirk saw a spasm of pain convulse his face. It seemed to deeply concern the dark, beautiful woman who was stooping over him. She touched his bald head gently before she hurried forward to greet the newcomers.

"Parmen and I welcome you to our Republic," she said. "I am Philana, his wife. Who among you is the physician?"

So the Platonians' philosopher-king was the patient. The startled McCoy said, "I am. What is the problem?"

She gestured to the couch. "You must do something. . ."

Following her, McCoy removed the covering from his patient's legs. An infection had swollen the left one almost to the knee. "What happened to that leg?" he said.

With a sick man's irritation, Parmen snapped, "What do you suppose? I scratched it!"

"I don't understand," McCoy said. "Why wasn't this attended to immediately?"

"Sheer ignorance. Is there anything you can do?"

The question put McCoy on guard. "We're certainly going to try. The infection is massive. Let me give you a shot to ease the pain."

McCoy opened his medikit; but before he so much as touched his hypo, it rose from the kit and sailing through the air, hovered for a moment. Kirk and Spock were looking up at it in amazement when Parmen said, "Where?"

McCoy came out of his shock. "Your arm," he said.

The hypo alighted on Parmen's upper arm, delivered the shot and replaced itself in the medikit. The sick man noted McCoy's expression. "Sorry, didn't mean to take matters out of your hands," he said. "But I can't risk any further contamination."

Watching, the dwarf touched Philana's white robe. "Mistress, they've come to help. They deserve better than to die."

Alexander had spoken so softly that Kirk didn't hear the plea. But what he saw was enough. The little man's mouth was forced open. His fist clenched and was shoved

163

into the open mouth. Then his teeth were snapped back to bite into his knuckles.

"Alexander, you talk too much," Philana said.

The fist was left in the mouth. Over it the dwarf's tormented eyes met Kirk's.

"What is your prognosis, Doctor?"

Parmen barely managed to utter the words. His breath was coming in heavy pants and he was perspiring profusely. But McCoy, scanning him with his tricorder, had not forgotten the hypo episode. "It will be better," he said, "if I handle my instruments myself without any help from you."

His patient stifled a cry of agony. McCoy took another closer reading of his tricorder's dials. As Parmen moaned, turning on his side, Kirk approached the couch. "I don't understand how a simple scratch could get this serious," he said to McCoy.

The *Enterprise* surgeon stepped to one side. "Neither do I. But it has. And how do I knock out an infection with a tricorder that has no information on Platonian bacteria? All I can do—and it's going to take time—is match his bugs with a known strain and *hope*."

"Look at the game board," Kirk said.

The dwarf's fist had been removed from his mouth. It had been removed so that he could play a game with one of the robed academician-guests. Kirk and McCoy saw Alexander move a piece; but his opponent's piece made its countermove by itself.

"Your pyramid is in jeopardy, Eraclitus," Alexander said.

A cube rose into the air and descended into another position. "Aha! It isn't now!" Eraclitus laughed. "I won the game."

Kirk went to Philana. "This psychokinetic power of yours is unique. How long have you possessed it?"

"Two and a half millennia—ever since our arrival here on Platonius."

Spock joined them. "How is the power transmitted?" he asked.

"Brain waves," she told him.

"Do these waves cease when you're asleep?"

164

"No, not if they're embedded in the unconscious," she said.

"How do dreams affect them?" Kirk said.

Her anxious face moved in a coldly formal smile. "Our sleep is dreamless."

McCoy, gathering chemicals from his kit, was mixing them in a vial. Delirium's symptoms were beginning to show in the twisting, fevered Parmen. Frustrated and disturbed, McCoy called to Philana. *Why don't you have doctors? Medicine?*

"We've had no pressing need for the medical arts, Doctor. While still on Sahndara, we instituted a mass eugenics program. We're the result. Pared down to a population of thirty-eight, we're perfect for our utopia. Overemotionality and concern with family have been eliminated. We're bred for contemplation, self-reliance and longevity." She paused. "How old would you say I am, gentlemen? Don't be afraid. I'm not vain."

"Thirty-five," Spock said.

"That old? I . . . I stopped aging at thirty. Anyway, you missed by two thousand years. I am two thousand, three hundred years old. We married very young, Parmen and I. I was only one seventeen, he was one twenty-eight. You see, we scarcely have to move any more, let alone work."

Kirk nodded. "That's why you have no resistance."

"True," she said. "A break in the skin or a cut can be fatal." She looked over at the couch. "We went for a stroll in the moonlight—something we seldom do—and my spouse fell . . ."

Parmen gave a cry. She hurried away from them to watch McCoy. He was working fast, pulling his mixed chemicals into the hypo. Suddenly a marble bust of Socrates fell from its pedestal, and the game board, along with its geometric pieces, lifted up and went spinning through the room. McCoy was trying to shield the hypo and vial with his body when he was whirled about and sent careening across the floor.

Kirk ran to help him to his feet. Spock, rescuing the hypo and vial, said, "Captain, I believe we are experiencing the psychokinetic manifestations of Parmen's delirium."

Kirk's communicator beeped. He flipped it open and

Scott's voice said, "Captain, we're fighting a storm! No discernible cause—I've never seen anything like it! Ten-scale turbulence right now, sir!"

As he spoke, the *Enterprise* gave a violent lurch. Scott turned to Sulu. "Emergency gyros and stabilizers at maximum!" To Kirk he said, "If it keeps up this way, we can't last, Captain!"

"Engines at full speed, Mr. Scott. Get her out of orbit and into space!"

"I've tried, sir. We're locked tight!"

"Then there's nothing you can do but batten down and weather it!"

"Right, sir . . ."

Kirk replaced the communicator in his belt. "Parmen's mind is not only throwing the furniture around, it's tearing the *Enterprise* apart! Bones, knock him out—and fast!"

McCoy drew the last of his chemical mixture into the hypo. He tried to hold his patient still long enough to administer it; but Parmen, staring at him wild-eyed, slammed him back against the wall. McCoy barely succeeded in hanging on to the hypo. Still in his delirium, the philosopher-king caught sight of Alexander. The dwarf was smashed against another marble wall.

"Help! Save me!" he screamed.

Unseen hands were pummeling the dwarf. They jerked him forward only to have him lashed again against the wall. He twisted, ran and was hurled once more against the wall. Kirk raced to him. Kirk seized him, shouting, "Stay behind me!"

"It's no use. His mind will find me anyhow . . ." He whispered, "Don't save him! Please don't save him. Let him die. The others will all kill each other trying to become ruler . . ."

A blow meant for Alexander grazed Kirk's cheek. "Bones, hurry up with that shot!"

McCoy, crouching too low for Parmen to see him, grabbed his arm and got the hypo home against his shoulder. Alexander was screaming again. "Agh . . . I . . . I can't breathe! Choking . . . chok—"

"Bones, shake Parmen! Break his concentration!"

As McCoy obeyed, emptying the hypo, the invisible

166

clutch released the dwarf's throat. A pedestal about to fall slowly righted itself. Kirk opened his communicator. Had quiet returned to the *Enterprise*?

"It's all right, Captain," Scott said. "The turbulence has abated."

"I think you'll find the orbit lock is broken as well. Assess damage, Mr. Scott, and repair what's necessary."

"Aye, sir."

Philana had seen that sleep had stilled the patient. Gracious now, she spoke to the visitors. "I don't know how I can ever thank you enough, not only for myself but for Platonius."

Kirk was brief. "No thanks are necessary."

"Alexander, show our guests to the South Wing."

"No, thank you," Kirk said. "We must return to the *Enterprise.*"

McCoy spoke. "Jim, I think I should wait till the fever breaks."

Kirk hesitated. He'd had enough of Platonius and Platonians. On the other hand, McCoy was a doctor. To snatch him away from a patient for whom still more might need to be done was arbitrary action, whoever the patient was.

"Then we'll stay," he said.

The South Wing was a magnificent suite, hung with silk and decorated in the same classic Greek fashion as Parmen's atrium. Alexander scurried about, introducing them to dressing rooms and sleeping quarters. "You need anything, just say so," he told Kirk.

Kirk smiled at him. "Thanks, Alexander."

"Think nothing of it; you people saved my life." He swallowed nervously. "I . . . I think I ought to tell you. . ."

"Tell us what?" Kirk said.

The little man appeared to change his mind. He shook his head, a worried little smile on his mouth. "Just that I didn't know any people like you existed."

Kirk peered through the door into an empty corridor. "Where is everyone?" he said.

"In their chambers—meditating."

Kirk turned. "Alexander, are there other Platonians like you?"

167

The dwarf's face quivered. "What do you mean, 'like me'?"

"Who don't have psychokinetic ability?" Kirk said quietly.

"For a minute I thought you were talking about my . . . my size. They laugh at my size. But to answer your question, I'm the only one who doesn't have it. I was brought here as the court buffoon. That's why I'm everybody's slave."

"How does one get this power?" Spock said.

"As far as I know, it just comes to you after you're born. They say I'm a throwback and I am. But so are you!" Fear came into his eyes. "I'm sorry. I didn't mean anything. I shouldn't have said that."

"Don't worry about it," Kirk said. "We're happy without the ability."

Alexander studied Kirk's face. "You know, I think you are," he said slowly. He paused. "Where you come from, are there a lot of people without the power . . . and my size?"

Kirk was beginning to like the little man. "Size, shape or color doesn't matter to us. And nobody has the power."

Alexander stared. "Nobody!"

Even as he stared, he was being pulled backward toward the door. He gave a miserable little laugh. "Somebody wants me," he told them. Then he was yanked out of the room.

Kirk looked at Spock. The Vulcan shrugged. "It will be pleasant to leave," he said.

Kirk began to pace. "That may not be easy. If Parmen should die . . ."

"Even if he shouldn't . . ." Spock said.

Kirk nodded. "This little Utopia of theirs is about the best-kept secret in the galaxy. Screening themselves from our sensors, locking us in orbit—*it all adds up to a pattern,* Spock—and one I do not like . . ."

McCoy, with his medical kit, came through the door. He closed it behind him.

"Well?" Kirk said.

"My concoction has actually worked. Fever's broken, and Lord, what recuperative powers! The infection's already begun to drain."

"Dr. McCoy, you may cure the common cold yet!" Spock said.

Kirk took out his communicator. "If we're going to make it out of here, this is the time." He flipped the dial. "Kirk to *Enterprise*. Scott, come in, please . . ."

"Scott here, sir."

"Standby to beam us up."

Scott spoke slowly. "I'm afraid I can't, Captain. All our instrumentations, even our phaser weapons, are frozen."

"The turbulence hit you that hard?"

"It's not the turbulence, sir. Damage to the ship is minimal."

"Then what's caused it?"

Scott's voice was despairing. "I wish I knew, sir. You tell me. I'm only reporting the facts."

Kirk eyed the door. It was still closed. "Scotty, we're up against a society that has psychokinetic energy more powerful than our machines. Did you get out into space?"

"No, Captain. The orbit lock is tighter than ever. And our subspace communication with Starfleet Command is completely severed."

Kirk spoke softly. The contrast between his voice and the fury in his face was so marked that McCoy and Spock stared at him. "I'm going to take care of this. I'll get back to you, Scotty." He closed the communicator, replaced it in his belt; and opening the door, strode out into the corridor.

He found Parmen sitting up on the couch. The philosopher-king's eyes were closed, not with weakness, but with the ravishment of aesthetic ecstasy. The deformed Alexander stood beside him, plucking a lyre as he chanted a song from an Aristophanes play . . .

Great Pan
Sounds his horn:
Marking time
To the rhyme
With his hoof,
With his hoof.
Forward, forward in our plan
We proceed as we began . . .

The wretched dwarf croaked, imitating a chorus of frogs.

He turned at the sound of Kirk's entrance. He seemed to shrink into a still smaller man at Kirk's approach to the couch.

"Your Excellency!" Kirk said.

Parmen opened his eyes, annoyed by interruption of his artistic trance. Then Plato's views on Republican behavior calmed him. "Parmen will do," he said. "Philosopher-kings have no need of titles."

"I want to know why the *Enterprise*'s weapons and instrumentation are frozen—why the ship itself is locked in orbit!"

"Captain, please. You're mistaken, I assure you . . ."

The bland evasion enraged Kirk further. "I just spoke to my Engineer aboard the *Enterprise*," he said. "We showed our good faith. Now you show yours. I want that ship released immediately."

Alexander, in panic, was shaking his head at him, mouthing the words, "No—no . . ." Kirk saw why. Parmen was manifestly displeased. The cultivated benignity of his face had been displaced by a supercilious tightness. "The amenities, Captain," he said. "Allow me to remind you that I am the head of this Principality. Guests don't come barging in here, making demands and issuing orders!"

He looked at Kirk's phaser. The weapon left Kirk's belt and zoomed into Parmen's hand. Kirk studied the cold face with contempt. "Guests!" he said. "You don't know the meaning of the word! Guests are not treated like common prisoners!"

Parmen was more than displeased by the rebuke. His face worked with rage—a rage that held no vestige of Platonic calm. "Don't take that tone with me!" he shouted.

Kirk's hand was lifted to strike him sharply across his left cheek. Then his other hand was brought up to slap his right one. In a matter of seconds he'd lost all power to control his hands. Parmen, leaning back on the couch, watched him repeatedly slap himself across the face with one hand after the other.

Control of his communicator seemed to be also lost. Despite several calls to Scott, he couldn't raise him. Finally, he closed the communicator. His face was burning from the beating he'd given it. Like his anger. That burned, too.

Spock turned from one of the silken curtains that draped a window of their suite. "Obviously," he said, "Parmen does not want any contact made with the *Enterprise*."

McCoy protested. "He may still need the ship's medical stores. Why should he prevent contact?"

"To hide any knowledge of his brutal treatment of a Starfleet Captain," Spock said.

Kirk shook his head. "No, Mr. Spock. One thing is certain. Parmen is not concerned with either my dignity or safety."

"Agreed, Captain," Spock said. "And he would not have treated you so brutally if he had any intention of releasing you—or the *Enterprise*."

Suddenly, McCoy rose from a couch and started toward the door.

"Where are you going?" Kirk said.

"I don't want to go, Jim—but I can't help myself."

As he spoke, Kirk was yanked toward the door, too; and Spock, twisted around, was forced to follow him. The three were literally trotted into the corridor, staring down at their moving legs in horror. Will-lessly, they were propelled back into Parmen's chamber. And to the beat of a lyre and drum. At their entrance, Alexander, a one-man band, evoked a great drum roll that matched the rhythm of their trotting feet. Parmen, Philana beside him, applauded the show.

She rose from the couch and curtsied to them. "Gentle spacemen, we are eternally in your debt," she said. "Please accept some trifles as tokens of our gratitude. They stem from the very source of our inspiration. To the noble captain, a shield carried by Pericles as a symbol of his gallant leadership . . ."

She motioned to a shield on the wall. It flew into Kirk's hands. He was about to drop it; but it hovered at his hands, persistent. At last he was compelled to take it; and Philana, smiling, said, "And to our silent and cerebral Mr.

171

Spock, that kathara from which to pluck music to soothe his ever-active brow . . ."

The instrument left a bench. It sailed over to Spock, who took it; and without looking at it, shoved it under his arm.

It was McCoy's turn to become the recipient of favor. "And lastly, the physician who saved Platonius and my spouse. To you, Dr. McCoy, that ancient collection of Greek cures, penned by Hippocrates himself . . ."

A scroll rose from a table and floated over to McCoy. Kirk saw him begin to unroll it. He took a furious step forward. "Has my ship been released yet?" he demanded.

Parmen spoke. "Captain, wait. I know what you're thinking. My humble apologies. You were badly used. In my own defense, allow me to say that my illness was more profoundly disturbing than I myself realized."

He leaned back on his couch. A great leaner, Parmen. From his newly-relaxed position, he added, "I'm sure, Captain, that you, too, have been out of sorts; and have reacted with fits of temper and rage. Unlike you, however, what I think and feel is instantly translated into reality. Please find it in your heart to forgive me."

Kirk said, *"Has the* Enterprise *been released yet?"*

"It will be, shortly. You're free to leave the planet."

Kirk turned on his heel, speaking over his shoulder. "Good day, then. And thank you for the gifts."

"Not at all. There is, though, one final request . . ."

Kirk whirled. He'd known there was a catch in this somewhere. "Well?" he said.

But Parmen was looking at McCoy. "After my nearly fatal infection," he said, "it has become clear to us all that we cannot afford to be without a skilled physician." He paused. "We'd like you, Dr. McCoy, to remain with us."

Kirk stood very still. He heard McCoy say, "I'm sorry. That's impossible."

Parmen sat up. "Your duties will be extraordinarily light. You'll be able to read, meditate, conduct research—whatever you like. You will want for nothing."

"I'm afriad the answer is no."

"We'd like to keep this cordial—but we're determined to have you stay, Doctor."

172

Kirk fought to keep his voice steady. "You can bring yourself to do this after Dr. McCoy saved your life?"

"I'm losing patience, Captain . . ."

Despite all his efforts, Kirk's scorn broke through. "And you consider yourself Plato's disciple!"

The comment amused Parmen. "We've managed to live in peace and harmony for centuries, my dear Captain."

Spock's voice was icy. "Whose harmony? *Yours?* Plato wanted beauty, truth and, above all, justice."

The remark hit Parmen where he hurt. "Captain, please! I admit circumstances have forced us to make a few adaptations of Plato. But ours is the most democratic society conceivable! Anyone at any moment can be and do just as he wishes, even to becoming the ruler of Platonius *if* his mind is strong enough!"

"And if it isn't strong enough, he gets torn apart like Alexander!"

Parmen reverted to another lean-back against his couch. "Oh, come now, Captain, we're not children. In *your* culture, justice is the will of the stronger. It's forced down people's throats by weapons and fleets of spaceships. On Platonius we'll have none of these. Our justice is the will of the stronger *mind*. And I, for one, consider it a vast improvement."

"Why?" Kirk said. "Never would we use our weapons for the kind of brutality you practice!"

Relaxation deserted Parmen again. He got to his feet. "Farewell, Captain Kirk."

Kirk spoke to McCoy. "Come on, Doctor."

He and Spock turned to leave. But McCoy was rooted to the spot where he stood. Kirk, looking back, saw him unmoving, rigid.

"Bones?"

"I—I can't move, Jim. They're going to keep me, no matter what. Leave, please!"

Before, Kirk had never understood the term "towering rage." Now he did. His fury seemed to be making him twelve feet tall in height. *"No!"* he shouted. "You're a doctor, Bones! They need your goodwill. They're just trying to—"

Parmen interrupted. "Captain, go while you still can."

173

"We're staying right here until Dr. McCoy is released!"

"This is not the *Enterprise*. And you're not in command here, Captain."

Kirk saw Philana shrug. "Why even discuss it, Parmen? Get rid of them."

"But that might offend the good doctor, Philana." An idea—a delightful one—seemed to strike Parmen. He smiled at Kirk. "You wish to stay? Then do, by all means. You can help us celebrate our anniversary." He spoke to the immobilized McCoy. "In the process, I hope we can persuade you to join our tiny Republic . . ."

McCoy's tongue was still his to use. "You won't persuade me," he said.

"I think we will," Parmen told him.

Two garlands detached themselves from a marble statue of Aphrodite; and, whirling through the air, landed at the feet of Kirk and Spock. They were forced to bend and pick them up. Their gifts fell from their hands; and the same force compelled them to place the garlands ceremoniously on each other's heads.

Parmen nodded to Alexander. The drum broke into a dancing beat. Kirk and Spock began a tap dance. Spock looked down at his shuffling feet in disgust. But Parmen's delightful idea of celebration was just beginning to be realized. The two *Enterprise* men found themselves childishly skipping around the pool, bowing to each other in mechanical precision. Then a line of a song was placed in Kirk's mouth. "I'm Tweedledee, he's Tweedledum . . ." Spock bowed to him, singing, "Two spacemen marching to a drum . . ."

It wasn't over. "We slithe among the mimsy troves," Kirk sang. Spock bowed to him again. "And gyre amidst the borogroves . . ."

The garlands were exchanged. Kirk pouted sadly at the loss of his; and Spock, grinning madly in triumph, put it on his head. They bowed stiffly to each other and were dropped to their knees.

"McCoy!" Kirk yelled. "You're not staying here, no matter what he does to us!"

Parmen made an imperious gesture. Kirk coughed. He

174

could feel the defiance in his face replacing itself with a pleading abjectness. He heard himself reciting—

Being your slave, what should I do but tend
Upon the hours and times of your desire?
I have no precious time at all to spend,
No services to do till you require.
Nor dare I chide the world-without-end hour
Whilst I, my sovereign, watch the clock for you.
Nor think the bitterness of absence sour
When you have bid your servant once adieu . . .

There was no time for breath. The shaming words continued to stream from him . . .

Nor dare I question with my jealous thought
Where you may be or your affairs suppose,
But, like a sad slave, stay and think of naught
Save where you are how happy you make those!
So true a fool is love that in your will
Though you do anything, he thinks no ill . . .

The idiot thing was done. Kirk's head went down. "Stop it! Stop it!" McCoy shouted.

Kirk looked up. "No matter what he makes me say, it's no. You hear me, McCoy—*no!* I . . ."

His head was almost twisted from his shoulders. He was jerked to his feet, an arm wrenched behind his back. Something grabbed him under the chin—and pulled his neck back, back until a cry of pain escaped him.

"Well, Doctor?" Parmen said.

McCoy was agonized, wavering with the torment of indecision. He was torn not only by laceration of his deep personal affection for Kirk. There was his professional obligation, too. As the *Enterprise*'s surgeon, its captain's well-being was his prime consideration. If he agreed to remain with these people, he could end the torture, serving both his love for Kirk and his duty to Starfleet service. Finally, he came to his anguished decision. He turned to Parmen. "I have my orders," he said.

Parmen's mouth tightened. "As you wish, Doctor."

Kirk was hurled to the ground. He got up, fists

175

clenched, and rushed at Parmen. The Platonian stared at him. Kirk was frozen, a raised foot still in the air. "Is this your Utopia?" he shouted. "You haven't even . . ."

He was flung again to the floor. Then words, too, were denied him. His vocal cords went dead.

"We've had enough of your moralizing," Parmen said.

McCoy whirled. "And we've had too much of *yours!* You will never get me to stay here!"

He was smashed backward.

"You will be happy to stay," Parmen told him. "It takes a little time, Doctor. But you will be happy to stay, I promise you."

He unfroze Spock from his knees. The Vulcan, sickened by Kirk's misery, moved toward Parmen only to be frozen in mid-stride.

Philana looked at Spock. "Perhaps you have been a bit too forceful, Parmen. There are other ways that might be more persuasive."

"I doubt that they will be as entertaining. But if you want to have a try, do so."

Spock gave a cry. Philana had sent him into a wild, stamping flamenco. He danced around and around the downed Kirk. McCoy, unseeing, was staring straight ahead.

"An excellent choice, Philana," Parmen said. He spoke to the rigid McCoy. "All you have to do is nod."

The air was filled with the clack of castanets. The viciously-heel-stamping Spock was moved in close to Kirk's head. An inch closer—and Kirk would be trampled to death. A stomping heel grazed his head. McCoy, about to make an appeal, clamped his mouth shut. Then he closed his eyes against the sight of Spock's helpless attack on Kirk.

The castanet sounds ceased. So did Spock's dancing. He froze in a finger-snapping gesture over Kirk's body. His arms dropped. He began to shake. Out of him came wild peals of laughter.

McCoy opened his eyes as he heard them. He looked, appalled, at Spock as his laughter grew wilder. He swung around to Parmen. "Mr. Spock is a Vulcan," he said. "You must not force emotion from him."

"You must be joking, Doctor," Philana said.

"It can destroy him," McCoy said.

"Come now," Parmen said. "There's nothing so wholesome as a good laugh."

Spock was battered now by the insane fits of laughter. McCoy saw him pressing at his chest to soothe the agony of the spasms. Kirk was fighting to lift himself to get to Spock. He sank back to the floor, too weak to do it. McCoy launched a fierce blow at Parmen. "You're killing Spock!" he cried.

"Then we can't let him die laughing, can we now?" Parmen asked.

The laughter ended. Slowly Spock fell to his knees, his head limp, arms dangling.

"The poor fellow does look rather miserable, doesn't he, dear wife?"

Philana encircled Parmen with her arm. "He does, dear husband. You know, nothing relieves misery like a good, honest cry."

McCoy stared at them. "He's a Vulcan! I beg you. . ."

Parmen's face was flushed with a growing excitement. "Later! Later!" he said impatiently. "That's probably not true of Vulcan men, anyway. Shall we test it, Philana?"

Spock's shoulders began to shake. His body rocked from side to side as though wracked by a sudden woe. He was looking into Kirk's pain-ravaged face. Kirk moved on the floor toward him, his arm out. "Hang on, Spock," he whispered. "Hang on! Don't let him break you open . . ." He was tense with the struggle to support Spock's repression. But it was no good. Spock's quiet face had turned into the tormented mask of tragedy. Tears welled in his Vulcan eyes and dripped down his cheeks. Unable to control his sobs, he crashed to the floor.

Alexander, trembling and outraged, hurried to the center of the chamber, his lyre in his hand. "Parmen! They saved your life!"

He was flipped back into the pool. He staggered up, soaking wet, his tears mixed with the water. From deeps he didn't know he owned, he delivered his final judgment on his society. "I'm ashamed to be a Platonian. Ashamed!"

It was a resourceful society. Kirk was lifted to his feet; and, from the pool, the dwarf was placed upon Kirk's back. Alexander's arm whipped him on as he was driven, skipping around Spock's body, its eyes vacant as Kirk passed him.

Parmen spoke sadly to McCoy. "How can you let this go on, Doctor?"

For the moment their ordeals were suspended. They'd been permitted to return to their suite. Alexander had followed them; and was now dressing himself in the dry tunic and pantaloons that were his buffoon's costume. But Spock, his eyes closed, sat apart. The total loss of emotional control had been such a violation of his Vulcan nature that he was still inwardly trembling. Kirk, resting on a couch, watched him anxiously. "Bones, can't you do anything for him?"

"There's no medicine that can help him, Jim. He has to get through this himself."

Despite his aching back, Kirk got up. As he crossed to Spock, McCoy joined him. They stood before him a moment, both quiet; and Spock, slowly becoming aware of their presence, opened his eyes. The awful experience of his turmoil was still evident in them. Kirk looked away from the painful sight of an overwrought Spock. He had no right to intrude on such private agony.

"I trust they did not hurt you too much, Captain."

"Just a sore set of muscles, Spock."

"The humiliation must have been hardest for you to bear, sir. I . . . I can understand."

He assumed his customary impassive expression. But it was belied by the tremor in his voice and hands. Kirk's fury flamed in him.

McCoy tried to be soothing. "The release of emotion is what keeps us healthy," he observed. "At least, emotionally healthy."

"Fascinating," Spock said. "However, I have noted, Doctor, that the release of emotion is frequently very *unhealthy* for those nearest to you. Emotionally, that is."

Kirk forced a chuckle. "Which proves again that there are no perfect solutions."

"It would seem so, Captain."

Spock's eyes closed again. He spoke with them closed. "Captain!"

"Yes, Spock."

"Captain, do you still feel anger toward Parmen?"

"Great anger."

"And you, Dr. McCoy?"

"Yes, Spock. Great hatred."

"You must release it somehow . . . as I must master mine."

Spock suddenly stood up, his eyes wide open. They blazed with rage. He shuddered with the effort to control it, his fists clenching. "They almost made me kill you, Captain. That is why they have stirred in me such hatred. Such great hatred. I must not allow it to go further. I must master it. I must control . . ."

He grabbed Kirk's arm. His hand tightened on it until it seemed his great strength would snap a bone. Kirk held absolutely still. Gradually, Spock relaxed. He dropped the arm. His body was quieted as though the fierce embrace of his captain's arm had been a desperately needed reassurance of the dear existence. He sat down.

McCoy, his face drawn with strain, drew Kirk aside. "Jim . . . Jim, listen. I've thought it over. This is senseless. I'm going to stay."

"You can't, Bones."

"I have Parmen's word that you'll be safe."

"Parmen's word! He'll let us beam up to the *Enterprise*—and then plunge the ship into this atmosphere!"

McCoy shook his head. "Why bother to trick me?"

"If he killed us outright in front of you, you'd retaliate. You're a doctor, you have the means." He put a hand on McCoy's shoulder. "I know you're trying to do the right thing. But if anyone of us got away, Parmen knows that Starfleet will never let this planet go unpunished. He dare not let us go. Sacrifice yourself by agreement to stay—and you'll only be signing our death warrant."

Alexander pulled at McCoy's uniform. "The Captain is right. I didn't warn you. They treated you like they treat me. Only you fight them . . ."

The dwarf's eyes filled with tears. "All this time I thought it was me—my mind that couldn't move a pebble. They told me how lucky I was that they bothered to keep me around. And I believed them. The arms and legs of everybody's whim. Look down! Don't meet their eyes . . . Smile! Smile! Smile! Those great people . . . They were my gods . . ."

He seized a vase; and, smashing it against a column, picked up a long, jagged shard of hard earthenware. "You made me see them!" he cried. "I know what they are now. It's not me, not my runty size! It's them. It's them!"

"Alexander, put that down," Kirk said.

"No! It's the best thing for them!"

Kirk and McCoy moved toward him. "I said drop it," Kirk said.

Alexander backed toward the door. "I'm going to cut them up. Parmen first. They'll become infected. Only this time, no matter what they say, let them die!"

Kirk nodded at McCoy. They both rushed the little man; and, as McCoy pinned an arm, the dwarf reluctantly surrendered the weapon to Kirk. "Let me at least give them a taste of what they gave me!" he pleaded. "Please! They're going to kill you anyhow! You already know that . . ."

"There's no point in your dying, too," Kirk said.

Alexander stared at him. Then a sob broke from him.

"That's . . . the first time . . . somebody's thought of my life before his own . . ." Remorse overwhelmed him. "But it's . . . all my fault. I should have told you right off that they were out to kill you. I knew . . . I knew—but I was afraid." The tears welled again.

"It's all right, Alexander," Kirk said. "We haven't given up. Maybe you can help us."

"I'll do anything for you . . . anything. Just tell me what to do."

"It might help us to know one thing. Did all the other Platonians always have the power?"

"No. Not before we came here to this terrible planet."

Spock had joined them. "Then they acquired their psychokinetic power *after* coming here," Kirk said.

"I guess so."

Spock spoke. "Is it possible for you to recall how long after you arrived here that their power began to develop?"

"How could I forget? It was exactly six months and fourteen days after we got here that they started pushing me around."

180

"Would you know how many months' supplies you brought with you?"

The dwarf's effort to remember was obvious. "I think it was four months . . . no, three. Yes, three . . ."

"That's close enough," Spock said. "Fascinating. The power developed two or three months after they started eating native foods."

Alexander's eyes widened in surprise. "Yeah! That's right."

Spock turned to Kirk. "Then it would be logical to assume that there is connection between their psychokinetic power and the native foods."

McCoy puzzled over Spock's hypothesis. "Then why wouldn't Alexander have the same power as the others?"

"Perhaps his system can't absorb the crucial element, Doctor."

"Bones, I'd like you to take a reading of Alexander's blood," Kirk said.

The dwarf clutched Kirk. "Will it hurt much?"

McCoy smiled at him. "You won't know it happened," he said as he ran his tricorder over his arm.

"Bones, you still have the tricorder reading of Parmen's blood?"

"Of course. Parmen possesses the highest order of psychokinetic ability; Alexander the lowest—and under the same environmental conditions." He looked at Kirk. "I'll put both of their blood samples through a full comparative test in the tricorder."

"If our theory proves out, we've got a weapon . . ." Kirk said.

When the tricorder buzzed, McCoy read out its information on its data window. "The one significant difference between Parmen's blood and Alexander's is the concentration of kironide, broken down by pituitary hormones."

"Kironide's a high-energy source. It could be it!" Kirk said.

"The pituitary hormones confirm the assumption," Spock said. He looked at Alexander. "They aslo regulate body growth."

"You mean the same thing that kept me from having the power made me a dwarf?"

Spock nodded. "It is obvious now why Parmen has

kept his Utopia such a secret. Anyone coming down here and staying long enough would acquire the power."

"Exactly, Mr. Spock." Kirk wheeled to McCoy. "Isn't there some way to build up the same concentration of kironide in us?"

"It'll take doing but it should be possible, Jim."

"Then what are we waiting for?"

McCoy went to work. Pulling vials from his kit, he inserted them in the tricorder. He checked a dial. Then he reached for an optical tube. More vials went into the tricorder. He hesitated. "Jim, even if the kironide has the desired effect, it still may not help us get out of here."

Kirk looked anxiously at Spock. "If all of us *do* come up with the power, what chance do we have against thirty-eight of them?"

"The point's well taken, Captain. However, the power isn't additive. If it were, with the Platonians' hostile propensities, two or three of them would have combined forces centuries ago—and deposed Parmen."

Alexander pulled at Kirk's sleeve. "He's right. Parmen says everyone has his own separate power frequency. He says whenever they try to put their power together and use it, it never works."

McCoy straightened, the hypo in his hand. "I'm ready."

"Then let's not waste time. Give us double the concentration found in Parmen's blood."

As Spock was injected, he said, "The time factor concerns me. It may take days or weeks before there's enough buildup from the kironide to do us any good."

"What about Alexander?" Kirk asked.

"Well," McCoy said, "since the kironide's already broken down and injected directly into the bloodstream, it should work on him as well as the rest of us. Better, in fact —he's acclimated."

But Alexander wanted no part of kironide. "You think the power is what I want? To be one of them? To just lie there and have things done for me—a blob of nothing! You're welcome to the power! And if you make it out of here, all I ask is that you take me with you. Just drop me anyplace where they never heard of kironide or Platonius!"

Kirk said, "All right, Alexander. All right . . ."

"Jim!"

At the tone of McCoy's voice, Kirk whirled. In the room air was shimmering with the familiar Transporter sparkle.

Unbelieving, he watched the dazzle form into the shapes of Uhura and Christine Chapel. They saw him—but when they tried to speak, their mouths were clamped shut. Then their legs moved, marching them like marionettes toward a dressing room.

"Nurse! Lieutenant Uhura!" Kirk shouted.

They didn't turn. As they disappeared into the dressing room, two lovely, sheer mini-robes floated after them.

Acidly bitter, Kirk finally spoke to his men. "The afternoon entertainment wasn't enough for them," he said.

And he stayed bitter, as arrangements were made for the evening's entertainment. *Enterprise* uniforms vanished. He and Spock were forcibly clad in short Greek tunics, knotted over one shoulder. Leaf wreaths were settled on their heads. And in the main room of the suite, a table appeared. Piled high with food, with fruit and wine, it glittered, heavy, with silver and crystal.

The dressing room door opened. A little shy in her highly becoming mini-robe, Christine hesitated. Then her pleasure in seeing them sent her smiling to them. "Are we glad to see you!"

Uhura addressed the question in Kirk's eyes. "We were forced into the Transporter and beamed down. It was like becoming a puppet for someone."

"I thought I was sleepwalking," Christine told him. "I couldn't stop myself."

"I don't understand it," Uhura said. "A simple invitation would have brought me running for this . . ." She lifted a soft fold of the golden robe that matched her exotic skin color.

"Definitely," Christine agreed. "Why use force on a girl to get her into clothes like these?" Then she paused, looking at Kirk. "Captain, what's wrong? Something's terribly wrong, isn't it?"

"Yes," Kirk said quietly.

He had heard the sound of laughter. The bewildered

girls stared at each other; and Kirk said, "Spock, have you felt any reaction to the kironide shot?"

"I have experienced a slight flush, Captain."

"So did I. Shall we try a simple test? Let's concentrate on raising that cluster of grapes."

They fixed their eyes on the grapes, the girls watching them in uncomprehending silence. The grapes continued to nestle placidly between two apples.

"Didn't budge," Kirk said.

There was a fanfare of music and a burst of applause. Kirk looked up from the disappointing grapes. Panels set into the room's walls had slid aside, revealing boxes behind them. They were crowded with Platonians. Kirk caught sight of Alexander at a music stand, his instruments beside him. Parmen, Philana and McCoy occupied the center box. The philosopher-king stood up, lifting a hand.

"Fellow Academicians! Twenty-five hundred years ago a hearty band of vagabonds arrived on this barren planet. Those were times of desperate hardship and heartbreaking toil. Then a divine Providence graced our genius with the power of powers! Through it, our every need was materialized. We determined to form a Utopian Brotherhood. This is a festive occasion. For tonight, we welcome its first new member into our Brotherhood!"

Kirk used the top of his voice. "Don't count on it, Parmen! First you must win the doctor's consent!"

McCoy, shouting back, called, "I'll never give it, Jim!"

Whispering, Parmen said, "Doctor, please. You are destroying the festive mood . . ." He waved a hand. "Let the madcap revels begin!"

The four *Enterprise* people were sent whirling around the couches in a game of musical chairs. Then Uhura was dropped on one in a languorous pose. Christine's turn came. Her chin was placed on a bent hand, her body disposed in a seductive position. Kirk and Spock were each pulled to a couch. After a moment they were caused to exchange places.

Eraclitus called from a box, laughing. "Ah, how fickle and faithless! Make up your minds!"

Spock sat on Christine's couch, straining against Parmen's will-to-power. It was no use. His arms encircled

Christine; and her hand was forced up to caress his face. The Platonians tittered.

"I am so ashamed, Mr. Spock." But even as her whisper reached Spock, her hand had reached into his hair to tousle it amorously. She whispered again. "Oh, stop it, Mr. Spock. Please make them stop it . . ."

But they were in a close embrace, Christine's arms entwined around him. His eyes were closed in desperate concentration. He was forced to open them in order to gaze passionately into Christine's. Their lips met. As the kiss ended, she said brokenly, "I have so wanted to be close to you. Now all I want to do is crawl away someplace and die . . ."

"Careful, Mr. Spock!" Eraclitus called. "Remember! The arrows of Eros kill Vulcans!"

Christine sank back on the couch. Spock's body followed hers to shouts of "Bravo! Bravo!"

Uhura was saying, "I am so frightened, Captain . . . so frightened . . ."

"That's the way they want you to feel, Lieutenant. It makes them think they're alive."

"I know it . . . I wish I could stop trembling . . ."

Kirk pulled her to him. Uhura looked into his eyes.

"Try not to think of them," Kirk said. "Try!"

She smiled faintly. "You know what I'm thinking, Captain?"

"What, Lieutenant?"

"I'm thinking of all the times on the *Enterprise* when I was scared to death. And I would see you so busy with your commands. And I would hear you from all parts of the ship. And then the fear would pass. Now they are making me tremble. But I am not afraid."

Her dark eyes were serene. "I am not afraid . . ."

They kissed.

The applause was scattered. And what there was of it was too loud.

Philana in her box stirred restlessly. "Parmen, let's get on with it."

"You are so impatient, my wife! Observe the doctor and learn. He is content to wait for the *pièce de résistance*."

Nevertheless, Parmen got on with it. He moved the

185

table of food into a corner and rolled another one into its place. It was loaded with weapons—swords, a bullwhip, knives, a battle-ax. In its center a brazier, a poker thrust into it, glowed red hot. The two *Enterprise* men were lifted from the girls' couches. Kirk found the bullwhip in his hand. He saw Spock reach for the poker. Its tip of iron flamed with its adopted fire.

Kirk whirled to the boxes. "You're dead, all of you!" he cried. "You died centuries ago! We may disappear tomorrow—but at least we're living now! And you can't stand that! You're half crazy because you've got nothing inside! Nothing!"

But Parmen was looking at the girls. Turning, Kirk realized that they had been transfixed, helpless, on their couches. The heavy whip rose in his hand and lashed out at Uhura. It flicked close to her cheek.

McCoy could bear no more. He rose in his box. "Stop it, Parmen! Stop it! I can't take any more! I can't! I'll do whatever you want!"

Apparently, his capitulation came too late. Parmen merely grinned at him. "I'll stay here with you!" McCoy cried. "I'll serve you. But stop this!"

Alexander broke from his place. Racing to the table of weapons he seized a knife and rushed at Parmen. He was stopped cold. Parmen stood up. "Alexander, again! He likes to play with knives. Very good. We'll indulge him . . ."

Slowly, relentlessly, the knife blade was pressed against the little man's throat. It halted there—and suddenly, unseen fists slammed Parmen against the back of his box.

The shaken Platonian stared around him. Staggering back, he shouted, "Who . . . who . . . who did that?"

Kirk tossed the whip away. *"I did!"*

Eraclitus was on his feet. "Impossible!"

"What's going on?" Philana screamed.

Kirk lifted his head to the boxes. "Platonians, hear this! The next one of you who tries anything will get hurt! Not only do we possess your psychokinetic ability, but we've got it at twice your power level!"

"Not twice mine!" Parmen's eyes veered to Alexander.

The dwarf was spun around; and, knife upraised, sent racing toward Kirk. Instead of evading the charge, Kirk stood still, drawing on all his strength of concentration. His new power slowed the onrush. With a supreme effort, he turned Alexander around and set him running toward Parmen. The battle of wills was joined. Parmen's cold eyes bulged with his struggle to recover control of the dwarf. But Alexander had picked up speed. He vaulted into the box, the knife extended to Parmen's heart . . .

The Platonian shrieked. "Captain, no! I beg of you. I'll do anything you say! I do not wish to die! Do you hear me, Captain?"

Kirk arrested the knife. But Alexander, so close to vengeance for his years of suffering, fought to plunge the knife deep into his tormentor. "Let me do it!" he cried to Kirk. "Let me finish him!"

Kirk strode to the box. "Do you want to be like him, Alexander?" he said.

The dwarf's eyes met his. After a moment, he shook his head. Then he threw the knife at Parmen's feet.

The new power was exhilarating. Kirk used it to force Parmen to kneel before the dwarf. Alexander looked down at the bald, arrogant head. "Listen to me, Parmen! I could have had the power—but I didn't want it! I could have been in your place right here and now! But the sight of you and your Academicians sickens me. Because, with all your brains, you're dirtier than anything that ever walked or crawled in the whole universe!"

As he jumped from the box to Kirk's side, he turned to say, "Get up from your knees! Get up!"

Parmen, his world crashed around him, spoke to Kirk. "Captain, you knew it was my intention to destroy you and the *Enterprise*. Yet you have spared me."

Kirk eyed him for a long moment. "To us, killing is murder—even for revenge. But I am officially notifying you that other Starships will be visiting Platonius—and soon!"

He'd been right. There was nothing in these people. Once their control power was defeated, they shriveled into nothing. Their ruler was too hasty with his reassurance. "There's no need for concern, Captain. They'll be safe. Of late, I've begun to feel that we've become bizarre and unproductive. It's time for some fresh air. We'll welcome your interstellar visits."

"I don't believe you," Kirk said. "The minute we leave, you'll lose your fear—and turn as sadistic as ever. So let me warn you. This incident will be reported in its entirety to Starfleet Command."

His voice went icy. "Keep your power. We don't want it. But, if need be, we can create it in a matter of hours. Don't try anything again."

All his essential weakness had appeared in Parmen's flabby face. "Understood, Captain. And you're right. None of us can be trusted. Uncontrolled power turns even saints into savages. We can all be counted on to live down to our lowest impulses."

"You're good at making speeches," Kirk said. "I hope your last one sinks in. Stand back."

Obediently, Parmen shrank back into the box. Philana was haggard, almost looking her great age. McCoy left them to join Kirk.

"Alexander!" Kirk called.

As the dwarf hurried over to him, Kirk released his communicator from his belt. Flipping it open, he said, "Kirk to Scott. I'm bringing a guest aboard. Standby to beam us up."

Alexander looked at him, love in his long-suffering eyes.

ABOUT THE AUTHOR

JAMES BLISH, author of Bantam's popular *Star Trek* series, once won the coveted Hugo Award for his novel, *A Case of Conscience*. He has written many other science fiction novels and short stories as well. Mr. Blish, who is trained as a biologist and was formerly employed by several large pharmaceutical companies, is an American citizen presently making his home near Oxford, England. He was one of three persons who jointly founded the famous Milford Science Fiction Writers'. Conference in the early 1950s, and, under the name of William Atheling, has written some of the most informed criticism of science fiction.

OUT OF THIS WORLD!

That's the only way to describe Bantam's great series of science-fiction classics. These space-age thrillers are filled with terror, fancy and adventure and written by America's most renowned writers of science fiction. Welcome to outer space and have a good trip!

THE EXCITING REALM OF STAR TREK

☐	2151	**STAR TREK LIVES!** by Lichtenberg, Marshak & Winston	—$1.95
☐	2719	**STAR TREK: THE NEW VOYAGES** by Culbreath & Marshak	—$1.75
☐	11392	**STAR TREK: THE NEW VOYAGES 2** by Culbreath & Marshak	—$1.95
☐	10159	**SPOCK, MESSIAH! A Star Trek Novel** by Cogswell & Spano	—$1.75
☐	10978	**THE PRICE OF THE PHOENIX** by Marshak & Culbreath	—$1.75
☐	11145	**PLANET OF JUDGMENT** by Joe Haldeman	—$1.75

THRILLING ADVENTURES IN INTERGALACTIC SPACE
BY JAMES BLISH

☐	10797	SPOCK MUST DIE!	—$1.50
☐	10835	STAR TREK 1	—$1.50
☐	10811	STAR TREK 2	—$1.50
☐	10818	STAR TREK 3	—$1.50
☐	10812	STAR TREK 4	—$1.50
☐	10840	STAR TREK 5	—$1.50
☐	11697	STAR TREK 6	—$1.50
☐	10815	STAR TREK 7	—$1.50
☐	10816	STAR TREK 8	—$1.50
☐	11285	STAR TREK 9	—$1.50
☐	10796	STAR TREK 10	—$1.50
☐	11417	STAR TREK 11	—$1.50
☐	11382	STAR TREK 12	—$1.75

Buy them at your local bookstore or use this handy coupon for ordering:

Bantam Books, Inc., Dept. ST, 414 East Golf Road, Des Plaines, Ill. 60016

Please send me the books I have checked above. I am enclosing $_____
(please add 50¢ to cover postage and handling). Send check or money order
—no cash or C.O.D.'s please.

Mr/Mrs/Miss_____

Address_____

City_____State/Zip_____

ST—1/78

Please allow four weeks for delivery. This offer expires 7/78.

Bantam Book Catalog

Here's your up-to-the-minute listing of every book currently available from Bantam.

This easy-to-use catalog is divided into categories and contains over 1400 titles by your favorite authors.

So don't delay—take advantage of this special opportunity to increase your reading pleasure.

Just send us your name and address and 25¢ (to help defray postage and handling costs).